T0083603

SEFER

MINGLING VOICES

Series editor: Manijeh Mannani

Give us wholeness, for we are broken.
But who are we asking, and why do we ask?
—PHYLLIS WEBB

Mingling Voices draws on the work of both new and established poets, novelists, and writers of short stories. The series especially, but not exclusively, aims to promote authors who challenge traditions and cultural stereotypes. It is designed to reach a wide variety of readers, both generalists and specialists. Mingling Voices is also open to literary works that delineate the immigrant experience in Canada.

Series Titles

Poems for a Small Park
  E.D. Blodgett

Dreamwork
  Jonathan Locke Hart

Windfall Apples: Tanka and Kyoka
  Richard Stevenson

The dust of just beginning
  Don Kerr

Roy & Me: This Is Not a Memoir
  Maurice Yacowar

Zeus and the Giant Iced Tea
  Leopold McGinnis

Praha
  E.D. Blodgett

Musing
  Jonathan Locke Hart

Dustship Glory
  Andreas Schroeder

The Kindness Colder Than the Elements
  Charles Noble

The Metabolism of Desire:
The Poetry of Guido Cavalcanti
  Translated by David R. Slavitt

kiyâm
  Naomi McIlwraith

Sefer
  Ewa Lipska, translated by Barbara
  Bogoczek and Tony Howard

SEFER

A NOVEL BY EWA LIPSKA

*Translated from the Polish by
Barbara Bogoczek & Tony Howard*

AU PRESS

First published in Poland as *Sefer* by Wydawnictwo Literackie, 2009
Copyright © Ewa Lipska and Wydawnictwo Literackie, 2009
English translation copyright © Barbara Bogoczek and Tony Howard, 2012
Published in Canada by AU Press, Athabasca University Press, 2012
1200, 10011 – 109 Street, Edmonton, AB T5J 3S8

ISBN 978-1-927356-02-9 (print)   978-1-927356-03-6 (PDF)   978-1-927356-04-3 (epub)
A volume in Mingling Voices ISSN 1917-9405 (print) 1917-9413 (digital)

Cover and interior design by Natalie Olsen, Kisscut Design.
Cover photograph copyright © HessenJense / photocase.com
Printed and bound in Canada by Marquis Book Printers.
Poem by Ewa Lipska "Drought" translated into French by Isabelle Macor-Filarska and
Irena Gudaniec Barbier

Library and Archives Canada Cataloguing in Publication
Lipska, Ewa, 1945–
[Sefer. English]
Sefer : a novel / by Ewa Lipska ;
translated from the Polish by Barbara Bogoczek & Tony Howard.
(Mingling voices, ISSN 1917-9405 ; 13)
Translation of: Sefer.
Includes bibliographical references.
Issued also in electronic formats.
ISBN 978-1-927356-02-9
I. Title. II. Title: Sefer. English. III. Series: Mingling voices ; 13
PG7171.I63S4413 2012   891.8'517   C2012-905427-5

Publication subsidized by the Polish book Institute, The ©POLAND Translation Program

We acknowledge the financial support of the Government of Canada through
the Canada Book Fund (CBF) for our publishing activities.

Assistance provided by the Government of Alberta, Alberta Multimedia Development
Fund.

PUBLICATION SUBSIDIZED BY
THE POLISH BOOK INSTITUTE
INSTYTUT KSIĄŻKI
THE ©POLAND
TRANSLATION
PROGRAM
©POLAND

Canada Council
for the Arts

Conseil des Arts
du Canada

**Government
of Alberta** ■

SEFER

"JAN SEFER, psychotherapist, resident in Vienna (Argentinierstrasse), insured with UNIQUA, adored by both women and men, distinguishing features: *Shabriri, Briri, Iri, Ri...*"

"Stop fooling about, it's a serious questionnaire.... What's that mean? *Shabriri, Briri, Iri, Ri?* A game from your childhood?"

"They're demons," I told Susanne, my plump colleague at the clinic where I worked three times a week.

"*Shabriri, Briri, Iri, Ri,*" she repeated.

"*Shabriri, Briri, Iri, Ri,*" I replied.

I liked it when she laughed. She had beautiful white teeth with orthodontic braces. Little clasps made of translucent sapphire glass. A thin wire held them together. I gazed enraptured straight into her mouth.

"How about going out for some demons some time? It's a kind of pudding. I must run, see you Tuesday…"

⌇ I had a remarkably original father. Father owned the Sefer publishing house, which, although it didn't bring in any income, helped him cope with his fear of depressive memories, and with claustrophobia. Fortunately he also worked at an historical institute — as a detective, because after all who but a detective can write history. He left behind an unravellable will, with which I'm still struggling today. I was an only child. In my youth I dreamed of becoming a doctor, a solicitor, a beggar, a musician, an actor, a demon, and a salesman. But I went along with the wishes of my whole family, read medicine, became a psychiatrist, and I practice psychotherapy now. Thanks to which, I became linked forever with the demons of our time.

In Argentinierstrasse I lived opposite Radio ORF and liked passing time in the café nearby. In the radio station's tiny shop I could browse through the catalogue of the very greatest concert recordings, adding to my collection of musical curiosities. The publishing house bored me rigid, but I was frightened of my deceased aunt. She would materialize from time to time, wagging her finger at me. The finger was a livid pink that resembled the cheek of a seventy-year-old acquaintance of ours who used rouge to enliven her complexion and correct her cheekbones. The rouge made me think of a ski jump, launching the evil spirits of our aging years into the void.

⌒ I drove into the cool, unfriendly car park. It was the start of a new year. The January Machine kept spitting bills and bank statements through my letterbox. I knew I had to buy a motorway toll sticker, check the stock market index, reread my patients' case histories, plough through the publishing house correspondence, pop into the printer's, and confront the calendar with the tearaway pages that lay obesely on my desk. A calendar fat with a whole year's excess weight, which it starts to shed on January 1. I already knew how it was going to end, the rate at which it would grow thinner, faster and faster, until anorexic December 31, my father's birthday. I have always had problems with that last page, it hurts, and when I finally throw it in the bin, I see my aunt again.

My preferred way to deal with the December days is to escape to the mountains, but first I would have to immerse myself in Internet offers, reservations, bank transfers. My brain's modularity makes me double-check the same thing over and over again. "Reboot your brain," Susanne would tell me, which was driving me mad. Nowadays everyone wants to apply computer terminology and concepts to the brain's complex and poetic construction: "Install a positive thought package. Search your memory engine. You have a virus in your program and it is recommended that you find the McAfee SiteAdvisor while surfing your imagination." "It's hard to make a sentence," my aunt used to say, "if there are no words."

⌒ The table where I'm sitting, the Italian art deco one — that's from my aunt. Rectangular, mahogany, one metre eighty centimetres long, ninety centimetres wide, on solid legs, "simplified complexity," the cut corners mitigate the sharpness of the rectangle. Its geometric mass is inlaid with a linear incrustation of ebony. When I was a child, I played it like a piano. I could hear its melting sound and everybody talking at once. My father was making funny noises: "*Goolia, Agata, Kata, Goliata*." Everybody twisted everything. Sometimes they talked in code. My aunt kept spooning sugar — which she didn't actually take — into her coffee. Round the table there were six plain and comfortable barrel chairs, which hundreds of people sat on. Sometimes there wasn't enough space. The guests brought leather bags, string bags, suitcases, boxes. They summoned memories. I remember ghosts, phantoms, and spectres.

At some point while I was studying psychotherapy, I was sitting at this table staring out the window. I already knew I was going to split up with my girlfriend. "You know, I'm going to South Africa for a long time, I don't want to tie you down," I lied through my teeth. But the window, the kitsch autumn, the rusty leaves, the intense variations on red, absolved me of everything. Beauty can excuse a lot of things, life proved later on. Cod on this table. Fried potatoes and green peas. "David," my uncle was telling my father, "I'm an atheist, but I think my energy must go somewhere." My aunt laughed as if she were starting up her own diesel engine, running on good desserts.

Father didn't like talking about his past. When I became a psychotherapist, I tried to persuade him. "It would help you deal with your emotions." "I don't have any emotions," he'd reply. At the clinic we'd sometimes give brain scans to patients if we wanted to study their most intense past experiences. Father treated me as a harmless maniac, my aunt ostentatiously read *Cure Yourself* or *Get to Know the Secrets of Your Own Brain* in front of me. "The greatest problems people like you have is with themselves. You're looking for yourselves in your patients. You like puzzles that grow into Freudian jigsaws. It always ends the way it should have started in the first place: namely, somebody inadvertently sleeps with somebody else, what's worse not in their own bed but in an aeroplane at thirty-five thousand feet; on top of that it's in their imagination, not in reality — which they mislaid at Madrid Airport…" My aunt licked her finger and, sure of herself, turned another page in the book.

But once I talked to my father for several hours. It grew darker and darker in the room, neither of us had the courage to turn on the light. "You know, I can't forget that day in the camp. A woman tried to hide her baby in a rucksack, and suddenly it started to cry. One German pulled a gun out and fired into the rucksack.

The crying faded, and I heard such a terrible shriek that it wakes me still today..." A moment later: "Go to Poland one day, to Kraków, I'll give you the street and the house number, the house might still be there." "Maybe we'll go together?" I asked. "No," he answered curtly. "That place, it isn't in me anymore." We said nothing for a while. I didn't even notice when Father left the room.

He had transferred that picture onto me, left me it in his will, planted it in my biochemical imagination. It seemed to me my hand was going numb, then I heard my aunt's voice: "Something must be burning." I smelt baking potatoes, and immediately my brain clicked in. We'll have baked potatoes for dinner, and I do so like them...What would I do without my comfort food?

I turned on the light. I turned off the light. I went to the kitchen, dense with the smell of baked potatoes. Father was reading *Die Presse* as if nothing had happened. Everybody was smiling and content. Although not a single one of them is alive now, I have that evening constantly before my eyes, and I say to them at the top of my voice: "Give me the biggest! The crispiest!"

But in my memory there's also the odour of mothballs.

Father told me how he hid in someone's wardrobe.

The Germans were running through the whole house. The wardrobe was stuffed with naphthalene mothballs and father began to choke. They had no trouble finding him, and it was a miracle he wasn't shot on the spot. From my father I've inherited a loathing of naphthalene; whenever I feel threatened, I sense that stifling, nauseating smell. Once my aunt took out her fur coat to air it and father said: "In the end that thing'll bite you to death." And he strode out of the house. "Let me know when it smells of mushroom soup in here."

$\backsim$ In the evening I went to the Musikverein, to a concert by Katia and Marielle Labeque: the Mozart Sonata in D Major for Two Pianos K448; Schubert's Fantasia for Four Hands in F Minor; Ravel and Gershwin after the interval. I'd subscribed for years. I'd sit right behind the orchestra, studying the conductors' faces, observing the work of the wind instruments, and the percussion, which almost hit me. It even seemed to me that I was part of the orchestra too, playing the role of a temporarily abandoned harp. I admired the conductors' grimaces of pain, weariness and rapture, the subconscious language of the face, sometimes I thought they were irrational deviations, behavioural signals. Even at such moments I couldn't escape my trade. And in the middle of the hall, I always saw my aunt. With a lorgnette. She was looking at me of course. She was there to conduct me, checking if my shoes were polished properly, if I was wearing the correct tie and shirt.

I couldn't take my eyes off the two thin French women, particularly Marielle who — finely tuned — merged with the piano and the blackness. She reminded me of an old flame, from a symposium in Amsterdam. It was on the theme of "Neuro-Mechanisms for Processing Musical Data." She worked in America, at a hospital in Durham County, North Carolina. We spent a long time talking in the Keizersgracht about the right cerebral hemisphere. The musical phrases located in our own right hemispheres conducted us from the Bonjour Restaurant into bed at the Golden Tulip Hotel. The thrill of listening to the music that we discussed with such intensity turned into high-speed love. My aunt, sighing: "Wine at noon is one of the things that expel man from this world."

During the interval at the Musikverein concert I bumped into my Polish friend. He had lived in Vienna for many years. His name was Benedykt, but we called him Benek. He introduced me to the Polish Embassy's cultural attaché, and we all drank a glass of champagne. After the concert we went to a café I loved — Café Museum. I used to come here with my father when he was still collecting old postcards and stamps. He was the guru of the group that met here. When he arrived, they always piled postcards and stamps in front of him. Father, extremely focused, made a selection. Everybody stared at him intensely as if the beginning or end of the world depended on his decisions. Occasionally somebody asked, "What's new?" or "How is the business going?" Father wasn't bothered about business, but he'd answer with a laugh: "Like matzos in Oberammergau." In Café Museum I'd sink into the cracked red leather armchairs and eat fruit ice cream. "Look," Father said from time to time, "this place is like Karlovy Vary," as if it meant anything to me.

My attention was fixed on an Alsatian lying under a neighbouring table and his leather-jacketed master, who looked as if he owned a Harley-Davidson. He was drinking beer and reading *Die Kronen Zeitung*, a newspaper our entire family despised. "You know," Father said, "Klimt used to sit at that table." I studied the empty table; there was a black ashtray on it, looking like my aunt's glove.

Now, after the concert at the Musikverein, we were

drinking red Burgenland wine. "You are in the land,"
I said to the attaché whose name I hadn't caught,
"where Mozart melts into chocolate and the Sonata
No. 10 in C Major resounds inside every praline." Then
we talked about surfboards and mountain trips. "Have
you been to Poland?" the attaché asked. I answered,
"Not yet." "Then consider yourself invited. After all,
we're all the same Europe now." And at that moment
I heard the sound of breaking glass. I felt a Rosenthal
wine glass had dropped from the hand of my aunt.

⌢ There had been fog in Vienna since morning.
Grey foam hung in the air. It started to rain. I remem-
bered the day of my wedding. One of the endogenic
episodes in my life. I was twenty-one, and I decided to
get married against the wishes of my whole family. Ida
was a university friend. We were in love, and Ida didn't
even protest when I read her chunks of Camus's *The
Rebel*. (Neurobiologists dealing with addiction problems
could say a lot about us.) Father summoned me for a
serious conversation: "You're making a mistake. But
there's nothing we can do here." On the wedding day
we drove to the Registry Office in Mödling, ten miles

south of Vienna, where Ida lived. It was raining. And to make things worse, the ignition system in my old Fiat broke down. We hunted for a taxi, Ida with a bouquet of drowned daisies and me in soaking trousers. A fire engine went past us, siren wailing.

"Maybe we should still think about this?"

"Are you insane? My family are here from New York, we've got dinner booked at Haas House."

Our shared umbrella bent itself inside out, it looked like my aunt's hat. She bought it once upon a time in England, at Newmarket race track, where a late friend of hers used to belong to the Jockey Club. We stopped a taxi, we slumped in the back seat, shaking off the remnants of water inside our mobile black tent.

"The Registry Office," I told the driver.

"Our car wouldn't start," said Ida.

"What make?" the driver asked.

"What make, darling?" Ida asked.

"Fiat," I said casually, making it clear I wasn't going to get involved in that conversation.

"Fiat! Who drives a Fiat nowadays?" the taxi driver mumbled to himself.

"What model?" he asked after a while.

"What model, darling?" Ida asked.

"Solaris," I answered.

"Never heard of it," said the driver.

"Never mind," I replied.

"Solaris? Really? Is that what it's called?" Ida inquired.

"That," I answered, "is what it's called." The ride continued in silence, which was a relief. As we were getting out of the taxi, I heard my aunt's voice: "Darling! Just look at them!"

Auntie eyed Ida up and down as if she were Rosabelle, Mary Queen of Scots' favourite horse. "I wouldn't bet a fiver on her," she told my mother later. "Wynken de Worde tells us a good horse should have three qualities of a man — courage, pride, stamina — three qualities of a woman — beautiful chest, beautiful hair, gentleness — three qualities of a fox — beautiful tail, short ears, good stride — three qualities of a hare — big eye, dry head, fast pace — and three qualities of a donkey — big chin, flat hooves, and high hooves." My aunt continued mercilessly: "As far as I can see, Ida only matches the last three."

I should add, though, that Ida was a slim, striking blonde and didn't like my aunt because she reminded her of her strictest math teacher. The ladies felt a mutual dislike at first sight, when the wind blew my aunt's hat off and Ida burst out laughing. Auntie fixed her with a homicidal stare, looked at the hat, then at me.

I dashed off in pursuit of it, but unfortunately we left the party before the dessert, because my aunt claimed she had a migraine. Ida never stopped laughing all the way home, insisting that the hat froze for a moment in mid air, as if deciding whether to abandon auntie forever. When I announced to her I was getting married, she said, "Buy land in a hurry, take your time picking a wife. She's pregnant?" "No," I answered. "So? Well?"

We divorced precisely a year later. We were two competing psychological subassemblies. The illusion passed as quickly as the effects of a psychedelic drug. I was beginning to carry the world on my shoulders, I had more and more frequent political headaches. Ida lived in a world of enthusiasm and she surrounded herself with (unjustifiable) applause. Sometimes it seemed to me she operated on only one cerebral hemisphere, the right one, susceptible to sudden and foggy ideas. "You're serotonin-deficient," she'd tell me. "Serotonin, serotonin," she kept saying. I was amazed when she passed all her exams as efficiently as I did. Now she works three hours away in Graz, the happy wife of a happy husband and with two good children. We meet sometimes and have the occasional coffee. And every time she repeats it: "Serotonin, serotonin."

We laugh at anything. Then I get in the car, switch on the Goldberg Variations, and breathe a sigh of relief.

⌒ In those days I often talked to my father. "Read yourself," he used to say, "read yourself carefully, revise yourself, then take the Test." Increasingly, his life was invading my space. Sometimes I felt he wanted to present me with some black box, the symbol of the disaster he'd survived. "Do you know what I'm going to tell the dead?" he used to ask me: "'I never forgot you.'"

I dreamed his dreams. Role-playing *Deadlands*, re-fighting the Battle of Gettysburg, I became hysterical. The slaughtered soldiers kept coming back to life and killing again. In all the corners of the world, everyone versus everyone. Ghost mines kept returning and with them silent miners in multiplying hordes. I was becoming lost in it, in some ghastly maze. I was terrified to move for fear of waking up the sleeping ghosts of history — like fairy tales ruled by sadistic fabulists. I'd stagger out of bed in the middle of the night. And smell the naphthalene.

∽ Father, to me: "You know the carpets in this room, we bought them in 1884." "A good year to buy carpets," I replied calmly. He looked at me sternly, and after a moment said, "It was 1984. You know that. You humour me like one of your patients." Here my aunt saved me: "Don't worry," she said, "all psychiatrists are insane."

I am sure the publishing house, in which he placed so much hope, prolonged his life. It mostly brought out non-fiction books, history, but novels and essays too. In the first years he often published authors from Argentina. There was some mystery in that, which I'm still trying to fathom. I know he had a few trusted friends there. Once he asked some help from me. From the Argentine Consulate he'd received the notebook of a German who had just died. It was a matter of checking names. I don't know the details of the case and I never will, but Father gave me a list of names and asked me to check them against the names in the notebook. He didn't want to deal with it himself, he said he hadn't time.

The notebook drew me in like a thriller. I drew up mysterious plots to go with each address and devised psychodramas. "*Norberto de la Riesta, funeral directors, Esmeralda 113, Buenos Aires…*" I was ravished by the language, round as oranges. I repeated it out loud:

"*Esmeralda, Esmeralda … Hotel Cervantes, Av. Rivadavia 19.*"
But then in *Av. Corrientes* something sobered me up:
"The Goethe Buchhandlung." Suddenly the oranges
weren't sweet and smooth any more, and I'd already
started writing a thriller in which Goethe became
someone's fake alibi. And then I found the Knut Ham-
sun Gesellschaft. Then the Trommler Orphanage.

I should add here that our Viennese flat was in
Argentinierstrasse — a sheer coincidence — which
added spice to the affair. In a dream I heard the words
of Pythagoras — "Everything is beautiful, thanks to
numbers" — as I stood facing the number 113. The
fact that there was no town or street or house in the
dream, only the number, was immaterial.

꩜ Many years later — Father was already dead —
a strange parcel came from Argentina. It was a humid
summer Saturday, the only day I used to devote to the
publishing house, which by then had folded anyway. I
looked at the clock on the wall, it was close to four. Type-
scripts were still flocking to our address and lay on the
desk like a heap of snow shoved in the gutter. But as
father used to say (after Martin Luther): "Thoughts are

tax-free, and only they are worth your time." I leafed routinely through the manuscripts and tucked them away in a cardboard box. I knew from my psychiatric practice that people need to tell their life story to other people. And whether it's a glamorous or tawdry tale, readers love to hitch a ride at the author's expense, to help themselves to a share of his despair or bliss while nibbling strawberries. But I was tired of the sunsets I'd read about hundreds of times. The same wind kept turning the pages, the protagonist was recycled too, I could easily write a monograph about him. Usually he was infected with loneliness and scoured the world around him for the source of his disease. Depression-inducing hormones plagued him; life felt to him like an isolation ward. Sometimes he was dependent on drugs or alcohol and then, oh so easily, he succumbed to the cult of writing.

I opened the next envelope. An Argentinean stamp caught my eye. It was a short letter: "Dear Professor ..." It was to my father. "I have not heard from you for years. As for our business, as you can guess time has done its work; they are either dead or down with Alzheimer's. I myself can't believe I'm seventy. I'm forwarding you a typescript that a rather strange individual gave me to pass on to you ... He sometimes did bits and pieces for

me, but I can't remember any more how I met him ..."
A long cream envelope was attached to the typescript
with a paper clip. Out from it I pulled a small sheet of
white paper folded double: *"My name is Elim T. I am a
hunter. For many years I have been hunting for my life. I am
sending you a fragment of my helplessness. I shall call you. . ."*

⌒ I poured myself a glass of wine, put on my
spectacles, and began to read. Soon I was drawn into
the magical geography of this short text.

Echoes of a Journey (into Poland)

I.

*He fell upon the little town, sudden as sin. On the hill
overlooking the forest he rented a house whose owners had
been living abroad for the past few years, with an aunt in
Buenos Aires. In their visitors' book they wrote: "Don't be
surprised if you find the lights are on in our house." He
registered his name: Al Tikrei. "Must be a Turk or some
foreigner, or a mason. Definitely not Polish. A Pole would
have a Polish name, wouldn't he? What's he doing in
our town, doing nothing?" "Apparently he was the devil's*

servant," the catechism teacher said in school. "A roadside angel," argued the hairdresser, because she always saw him running in the road, totally immortal. Sometimes he dropped into the Albatross Bar and drank red wine. He ate fog: somebody from town saw him. The chemist said he had trouble with insomnia. He often bought melissa leaves, madder, motherwort, St. John's Wort, heather, primrose, elderflower. Fifty grams apiece. There were many theories about that. He talked strange. An excess of meaning halfway through the sentence ... You can't make head nor tail of it. For instance: "The trees aren't standing upright, that's only how we see it." He said that once. The townsfolk kept saying: "If anyone ever looked like a heathen, he does. People like that are always lucky." A few also saw him talk to himself. But they couldn't hear anything. "He was stealing our space."

2.

The parish priest learnt from a certain bishop that "Al Tikrei" in Hebrew means "Do Not Read." The priest told this to the fire brigade chief while playing patience. He begged for discretion. "The bishop explained, it's inexplicable. It's called the 'exegesis technique.' Psalm 62, verse 12: 'Our God has spoken once; and twice have I heard it.'" "If I shouted it from the rooftops," the priest finished, "no one would believe me." The fire brigade chief revealed this inadvertently

during the forest fire. The priest proclaimed from the pulpit:
"Turn back from the path of evil. When you reach the
recycling bins (glass, metal, and paper), take the turning
to the church ..."

3.

The spirit of A.T. hovered over everything. There was the
question of his faith. He was never seen in church. Can he
be saved? "Yes," said the priest, "if he doesn't doubt God's
charity." Then the scandal broke out: his entire right side
was an atheist.

4.

He decided to give a talk in the town; they took emergency
safety measures. They called an ambulance plus the police
inspector, the priest, the mayor. He began: "What does the
Talmud say? Seven things were created before the world.
They are the Torah, contrition, Paradise, Gehenna, the
throne of glory, sanctuary, and the name of the Messiah."
The chemist's daughter fainted. The uncertainty spread
with the sighing of the willows. "And if you die" — the
speaker plunged them into darkness — "with no time to
condemn your sins, what will be your chances after death?
You have no chance. You'll be swept by a wave like a tree
pulled out roots and all. A dead flag of leaves."

5.

After that no one saw him for a long time. Out went the lights in the house on the hill. You can't predict anything, they said. We don't know life by heart. Apparently he appeared to someone on the television. Otherwise, everything went on as usual.

6.

Somebody said he left a doorknob on the table. They asked, "Why a doorknob?" A.T.'s absence was treated like a sleight-of-hand trick. He was, and now he's not. Were we inhospitable?

7.

Something's wrong if it's dawn at sunset.

"The important thing is," A.T. said on one occasion, "What letter does it start with?"

What letter? The police inspector was suspicious. Can a statement like that be unpremeditated? Are there any witnesses? What does the priest say? The priest was silent and watered his ferns.

Then Al Tikrei asked: "Why does the story of the world start with the letter Bet?" And leaving the question unanswered, he left the town.

"Who was he asking?" the commander wondered, "Probably no one, because what's the point of talking about

the beginning of the world, when people are prophesying the End. And the Next World, what will that be like? And will it always be Next?" The inspector opened the police station window and stared into the sombre void of the town. An unfair fog lingered over it. On the wall of the Iskra sports stadium somebody had scrawled:

"Gas the Germans and the Jews."

At that moment I heard a sharp knock on the door.

"What about all the rubbish, Herr Doktor? Should I take it?"

"If you'd be so kind," I said to the caretaker, "It's papers."

"And what's it come to, Herr Doktor, they're scaring us with this recession."

"Don't worry too much, it's curable. I recommend green tea."

I liked her indiscreet laughter, which revealed her matter-of-fact attitude to living. She used expressive words with a dash of Vim and she smelled of Tropical air freshener (it's for cars). I slipped back into the intriguing text.

8.

It was the beginning of the fifth day of the week. The post office clerk was stamping letters. The postman stood in the doorway and studied the clerk's small hands. Then he sighed:

"Life's unpredictable …"

9.

The clerk stopped her work, looked at the postman and said:

"But that's why my marriage collapsed. I predicted my husband's death."

"What? Your husband's alive, isn't he?"

"Exactly. We were young, healthy, and in love, then one night I dreamt I was in mourning. All that remained of my husband in my dream was his absence. I woke up in fear and trembling. He was still lying next to me. It seemed to me he wasn't breathing anymore. I tugged at his hand, and I couldn't believe it when he suddenly jumped up, asking what had happened. Had something happened? Ludicrous question, isn't it? I began to cry a lot. I was weeping for him. With every knock on the door, I expected a Notification of Death. Meanwhile he kept on going out to work. And coming back. I cooked him cranberry compote but behaved like a widow. I started buying black dresses, blouses, jackets. We began living a life after death. Something had to happen, I knew. Because it was all predicted. One day my dead

husband, whom I so adored, applied for a divorce at the district court ... I don't even know where he's buried."

She confirmed it by stamping another letter.

The postman asked, "Isn't this work boring?"

"No. Why? There's a different date stamp every day."

10.

Late that autumn, the owners of the house on the hill overlooking the forest unexpectedly returned. It was raining.

"Do we ever wonder why the rain falls?" the chemist's daughter asked nobody as she stood in the chemist shop doorway, watching streams of hydrogen oxide flow down the glass. A black Peugeot estate car moved slowly on the muddy road. The headlights penetrated the dark, pushing damp blackness aside. Everybody saw it drive through the town, then turn towards the forest. The chemist's daughter swore there was no one inside.

"It drove itself, and it looked like a hearse. A bit later, the lights turned on in the house, but then they switched off straight away."

The pages of the *Echoes* were accompanied by another letter, which seemed like part of them:

*Thank you for letting me spend these few, inevitable, months
in your house. An acquaintance of mine, your friend, had
recommended the area. As he always said, it's ideal for lazy
mystics. My parched soul wanted to write a book. About love.
And tears. "They say he cried as he kissed her ..." I wrote
at the rectangular table with the thick linen burgundy
tablecloth. If you remember, there was an album on it.
Photographs guard the past, so I suspect you left it there on
purpose. For the first few days I just admired its presence.
Is it right to become an accomplice to somebody's life? By
joining a funeral procession that's just passing by? But then
one evening I decided to make fishcakes,* pulpety rybne,
*for supper. I mixed some chopped cod with finely cut lemon
zest, oregano, soaked bread, salt and pepper. I added two
eggs and shaped the fishcakes. Just like my mother used to
make. I poured oil into a shallow pan, fried some chopped
onions lightly, added water. I placed the fishcakes in the stock.
I prepared a lemon sauce separately, from lemon juice and
egg yolks, adding saffron and chopped parsley. I opened a
bottle of dry white wine and — please forgive me — I took
the album in my hand.*

*The first photograph resembled a yellow desert. A woman
in a hat. A man in a hat. With a moustache. A little girl
with a bow. Caption: "My parents and I, Karlsbad," date
illegible. Then more. A slim brunette. Without a hat. Two*

little girls. Possibly a boy and a girl. Then a woman, but much younger. In a dark dress. Against the background of a funeral parlour. The sign: Norberto de la Riesta. A laughing priest. Sinado Evangelico. Caption: Esmeralda 162. A street. Caption: Rivadavia. A young man walking north. Lighting a cigarette, but as if he were hindered by a strong west wind, the pampero. It was unbelievable, the news that awaited him in the flat, in 14 Plaza de Mayo. News full of contradictions. There was a toucan sitting on the window sill. Please forgive me if I leave an air of uncertainty. It's my inheritance from my antiquarian granddad and from years of examining the core of things.

The letter was signed carelessly and illegibly. I put away the typescript. I studied the envelope again. Grey, smooth, with the postmark smudged. *Plata . . . del Plata.* . . . Forty pesos.

I stayed in the office till late that night. What I'd read left me restless. I wished I'd talked with my father more about his Argentine connections. Years after the event, when we want to know more, when we want to understand time past, it's already too late. Time past's already in the other half of the hourglass, buried forever. My thoughts were like tourist trails in the mountains, uphill here, downhill there, steep slopes, twists, the valleys eroded. The neurone cables led nowhere. "Could I stop breathing?" a patient asked me once, "Could I stop breathing just because I don't want to be alive?" "Could I stop breathing just because I don't want to be alive, while at the same time I long for it so much?"

༼ꔷ The Argentina motif came back to me a year later. Somebody phoned me, apparently the man who sent the letter. He already knew my father was dead but so, he wanted to tell me, was the author of the *Echoes.* "He died in a car crash, in a little town called Jesús María, it's fifty kilometres from Córdoba. Why did he go to Jesús María? To meet Fate? And you, have you ever been to Argentina? Never? Then you know nothing. Have you ever danced the tango? Do you even know the music? You know nothing. If you haven't been to Argentina, you know nothing. The music, the dance, what it feels like listening to Carlos Gardel, León Gieco, *si*, there's no way. You have to come here and live through centuries of nights thick and sweet like dark chocolate, like nostalgia. What can you know about nostalgia? If you haven't been to the end of the world, you know nothing. And he went to Jesús María. For what? There was a note in his room, on the table: 'I am leaving my biography at the *poste restante.*' We'd all like that, yes? To leave our biography at the *poste restante.* Wouldn't you? You have got to come here!" His torrent of words flooded over me, but suddenly we were cut off. He didn't redial. He never phoned again. It seemed to me he had wanted to tell me that the *Echoes* didn't really exist, that it was just a joke, perhaps an attempt to describe something that could not be described. Perhaps this was just the helplessness of authors, for how many novels can you write, how many words, moods, and sunsets can you use?

The novelist Stanisław Lem, when he still lived in Vienna, in Hietzing, once told my father that every new book pushes one that was published earlier into a giant bin. We were amused at the time by this comic version of the history of literature. As we said goodbye to his nice family, we were carrying — instead of discarded novels — a huge basket of plums. I still remember their size, their taste. Sometimes my aunt would make povidel plum spread and misquote Cervantes, saying, "There's no better minister for love than some plum marmalade."

⌒   I was sitting with Doktor A., a friend from the hospital, in a bar in the Bermuda Triangle (that's in Schwedenplatz), discussing the bondage of memories, Glenn Gould, Thomas Bernhard's *The Loser*, and homemade preserves. The larder of my childhood was piled high with pyramids of jars and bottles: marinated mushrooms, pickled gherkins and mixed vegetables, pumpkin, beetroot, plums in vinegar, bottles full of tomato purée and sorrel. When a tomato jar exploded near me once, my aunt kept repeating, "It's no reason to boast and nothing to be proud of."

Doktor A. and I had similar childhoods and similar larders. We were both amazed by the talent of Glenn Gould and we wondered whether he really suffered from Asperger's Syndrome or was only an eccentric genius. We both liked to listen to the records with him singing in the background. Doktor A. told me all about his women, unfulfilled love, sex: "Two people, flabbergasted by each other, speaking the same romantic dialect, climbing the Mount Everest of love together, and then suddenly lost in the fog of ambivalence. I often talk to my patients about it, but I have problems I can't deal with myself." Looking hungrily at a dark-skinned waitress he murmured, "What's the price of love?" "Stocks are falling," I said, "the recession's begun. Invest your emotions in short-term accounts, it's safest." Sipping grappa, we laughed carelessly.

⌒ My atheist father used to say, "God always goes on holiday at the most inappropriate moment. In the face of a disaster, he'll flee the scene of the accident." Sometimes we used to go to Prague, a city Father liked a lot. Before the War, the *Numerus Clausus* was in operation in Poland — only so many Jews could go to college — and so my father studied history in Prague. He never forgot *drštková* soup, some sort of tripe plus paprika; it's almost unknown in Austria, and it's disconcerting. We stayed at the Hotel U Koruny, walked along the Vltava, and Father summoned vanished places that suddenly crowded in from all over like packs of lost dogs. Time was falling with the rusty leaves. We visited philatelists' shops, Father still had his old friends there, he bought stamps and postcards. In Prague I could see the child inside him, fragrant with love and an impossible enthusiasm for life.

⌒ "So," I said to Susanne, "Let's talk about demons."

"*Shabriri, Briri, Iri, Ri*, Herr Doktor."

"*Shabriri, Briri, Iri, Ri*," I replied. "Guess what, at night you mustn't drink water from rivers or ponds. Especially on Wednesday or Saturday. But what if you're parched? Shabriri will get you. Then you must say: 'Beware of *Shabriri, Briri, Iri, Ri!*' So now we can safely drink our Cabernet Sauvignon from Bordeaux."

We were out for dinner. My plump colleague looked at me uncertainly.

"Sounds like a code," she said.

"We all have codes."

"I don't," she protested strongly.

"That's what you think. Everybody's got one. It'll come to you, you'll see."

We were eating *Tafelspitz* in my favourite restaurant, the Hietzinger Bräu, while planning our work for next week.

"You know, my boyfriend's got some problem he won't talk about. Obviously I'm suspicious, and I'm starting to think he's going to break it off. He denies it, he says he loves me."

"Oh dear, he says he loves you? Your introvert boyfriend?" I already knew him from Susanne's stories. "And you're sending him warning signals, right?"

"What do you mean?"

"Medium-range ballistic missiles. You're trying to beat his defence mechanism."

"Don't make fun of me."

"*Shabriri, Briri, Iri, Ri.*" We clinked glasses. My right hand, her left. The asymmetry suited us nicely. For a while longer we talked about the Introvert, about everyday banal realities, about incest and *Punschtorte*, which we sinfully ate for dessert. Then we were absorbed into the thick blackness of the night, I drove Susanne home.

In the car park lift I bumped into a neighbour coming back from the sauna in our building. Flushed and warm, she worked on me like an unusually exciting radiator —"The elevator of bliss," I thought — and when we said goodnight the lift door slid shut behind me like a lascivious curtain.

⌒〇 I was slowly making up my mind about going to Poland. Sometimes my aunt appeared to me in hat shops. She'd peek out from behind her veil and wave at me, smiling ironically: "You've got to do it for your father." I gazed into shop windows full of woolly balaclavas, the hit of the season and a portent. I began looking up my Polish friends more often. I understand Polish quite well, but the speaking's harder. I even phoned a school friend. He lives in Switzerland but his family originally came from a little town in Eastern Poland, near Lublin. And just a few days later, there was a letter from him:

"I ended our phone conversation so abruptly, I'm sorry. And I'm sorry I haven't written till now. But guess what, I have been through a year of total de-humanization. This was due to bona fide Depression, involving a clinic rather like the one you work in, except that it's set in the beautiful gardens of Zurich. I've been through apathy, pills, physical torture, anxiety, and God knows what, followed by a Total Recovery. I thought about you a lot, dreaming of you coming and chatting about *taedium vitae*, like we used to. As for your tremulously-expressed scheme — to visit *Polska*, I find it hard to comment. It's like the joke. There's a lunatic stuck behind bars inside a basement cell. One day through the window he sees a man's head and torso, which then disappear, suggesting the man must have squatted down. When the body parts reappear, the lunatic asks: 'Excuse me, but what are you doing?' Comes the reply: 'I'm putting shit on the strawberries.' 'That's odd, I have them with sugar. But then I'm a lunatic.'

"In other words I am hardly a credible expert on Poland, given my immersion here in Switzerland's blend of total archaism and modernistic hi-tech. I'm allergic to Poland. Several reasons: (a) Legendary INNOCENCE of 100 percent of the population (see Dostoyevsky); (b) No sense of THE PRESENT; (c) Unbelievable PROVINCIALITY; (d) Lack of TARGET SPACE, i.e., scope for individual social participation; (e) Popularity of patricide (especially if Dad catches you spending his money on a greenhouse), using the *Teach Yourself English* book stuffed in your gumboots... I am not sure how you're getting on with Eros, but do steer clear of chance encounters with Polish ladies (who by the way won't seem too attractive unless your taste's on the crude side). Anorexic cosmetics-drenched girls can be found in the company of provincial Don Juans (often local councillors); women of my (shall we say 'middle'?) age tend to be sour, tense, traumatized, and the spitting image of my mother-in-law. But me, I'm a lunatic and I might be wrong..."

He's not changed a bit, I thought, grinning at the letter. He was always different from the rest of us. Isolated, depressive. "I've just invested my depression in some real estate," he wrote to me once.

⌒ Once a month Pani Róża came round to clean the flat and iron the shirts I hadn't managed to iron myself. "I found her on eBay," Doktor A. told me. "She's Polish, but she's lived in Vienna for a few years. She's working illegally." Pani Róża turned out to be La Bella Rafaela as painted by Tamara Lempicka. She had a square face, short dark hair with the fringe falling carefully over her low forehead. The shy look she cast on me concealed her eccentric, androgynous, decadent character. She didn't talk much, was polite and hard-working. Usually I left her the keys and went out to the café nearby to look through the morning papers. But there were days when I wanted to talk to her. Surprised, she'd stop work and answer my questions in a low, velvety voice. "Róża, what are you saving up for?" "For a flat. But the prices keep rising and I keep working." I knew she went to meet her friends in Rennweg, near the Polish church, and after Mass they'd all go for a beer at a nearby restaurant. She rented a room in Lessinggasse with four other friends, and once a month she went by coach back to Poland to visit her parents and her fiancé. "Fiancé" — she stressed the word proudly. I listened to all this as if to the script of a soap opera about our New United Europe. And how did Pani Róża's Viennese work trips impact her chemistry? The role of economics in neurology and neurophysiology has always fascinated me. I was about to finish an article, working title: "Psychic Doping in the Age of Globalization."

⌒⌒ Before I went to Poland I went to dinner at Doktor Benek's. He lived in a beautiful corner of Vienna in Schiller Square, with a view of the Art Academy. As I drove, I listened on the radio to Jacques Loussier playing Bach. It was coming up to 6:00 p.m., I still had to buy a bunch of flowers for Benek's wife, Teresa, and find a parking space, which isn't so easy in that part of town. When Loussier reached Prelude no. 1, I suddenly felt infinitely lonely inside the box of my car. I like this kind of loneliness, domesticated and melodic, which comes to me most often in concert halls or while searching fruitlessly for a place to park. The bad kind, which I'd compare to lipoproteins, descends on me like a migraine. Then I'd often reach for my beloved Tranxene. "Why don't you marry her," said my aunt, the enemy of all medicines: "No one else has married a tranquilizer yet. A wife like that's a treasure. Every night you just swallow her and that's it. Marry her!"

After about fifteen minutes of driving in circles
I finally found a space. I bought some yellow tulips,
which will always remind me of my Amsterdam fling,
and made my way to the Beneks. I am always amazed
by their flawless attention to detail. Benek, sumptuous
and scented, as if on his way to a concert at the Metro-
politan Opera; Teresa in a black dress, beautiful, languid,
absent, with artfully tired eyes, like the sensuous Psyche
in Simon Vouet's painting. A naked winged boy circled
round her the whole evening. Bisexual melancholy filled
their sumptuous lounge. I admired Benek's white leather
sofas and armchairs, and a crowd of crystal glasses that
splintered light into pieces. I adored Benek's cousin
Margot. She reminded me of my aunt and I admired
her unending flight from implacable Time, which was
chasing us all. She was prepared to rip the hands from
the symbolic clock and leave it ticking in amazement;
sooner or later it would have to stop.

"Gin and tonic? You haven't changed at all," said
Benek, pouring the drinks. "How do you do it?"

"There's a beauty salon in Graben he goes to three
times a week," Margot laughed.

Just what my aunt would have said.

"A beauty salon in Graben? Not at all, it's a face lift
in a garage," I answer.

I can hear Margot's voice. "You know, Teresa, Armani this spring's going to be white, ecru, light blue. Even draped chiffon."

Teresa's looking at her with absolute approval.

I throw in: "A sensual collection, satin silk."

"And how do you know?" Benek asks.

"From my ladies."

"Have you read the new Robert Menasse?" Margot quizzes me.

"Not yet," I say, ashamed.

Benek's cousin is always up to date; cultural current affairs, next month's Concert Hall repertoire, scandals, the new gossip, everything we love talking about at social events.

"Were you at the concert? Why didn't we get together in the interval for a glass of champagne?"

"The crowd was too big." Teresa served a starter: a salmon-wrapped egg.

"My Mercedes is acting up," Benek tells me.

"Then get a Toyota. I've been driving one for four years, no trouble." I say it loudly, though I know that in his case it's inconceivable. Benek's Mercedes is his extra hormone. Oxytocin, hormone of happiness and love.

Then we discuss horsepower, gear boxes, hybrids, the latest play at the Burgtheater, the Klezmar concert

at the Konzerthaus, and other boosts to the imagination.
Then we have genuine Polish cheesecake for dessert
and that's when I dare to say:

"I'm going to Poland."

Silence falls. Benek breaks it first:

"At last! That's incredible!"

"What's happening there?" Margot asks. "A conference?"

"Something like that."

"Kraków?" Benek asks and he takes out a bottle of
champagne.

"I'm driving, don't open it."

"You don't need to drink the whole bottle, but we
have to celebrate. Planned everything?"

"More or less."

"And where," Benek asks, "will you stay?"

"I stayed in a little hotel in Długa Street," Margot
throws in.

"He won't be staying at any little hotel in Długa
Street."

"And why not?" Margot continues, "It's decent
enough."

"Forget Długa Street, you can't call that a hotel.
Possibly," Benek ventures, "the Holiday Inn."

"Oh, that's a great hotel," Margot scoffs, "for third-
rate businessmen."

"The Rose Hotel," I can hear Teresa from a distance. "It's central."

"Even the Grand would be better," Benek adds.

"Perhaps a guest house —" I begin, diffidently.

"Are you mad? They'll rob you," Margot gets started. "How do you know what kind of place it is, it might be a brothel."

"His dream come true, my dear."

"Well, in that case …" Margot gives up.

"I know," Benek exclaims, pouring the champagne. "The Hotel France, that's central too."

"Yes, someone's recommended it to me already," I say.

"Are you flying?" Margot asks.

"No, I'll probably drive."

"You know how they drive there? How many people die in a week? We only fly these days."

"They drink and drive."

"Just like me when I leave here," I say.

"Do you know what their roads are like? You'll lose all your teeth," Margot jokes.

"Then I'll get new ones. I haven't liked mine since the day I was born."

⌒⌒   The Argentina motif resurfaced when I heard my friend Doktor A. was going to take his children on two weeks' holiday to visit their Polish-Argentinean relatives.

I invited him to a bravura veal roast in béchamel sauce, and I showed him the typescript I'd received. "I'm sure the man who phoned must have been sending my father information, about Germans hiding there after the War." "I think the guy was also searching for someone off his own bat." "At some point he must have gone to Poland." "*My name is Elim T. I am a hunter. For many years I have been hunting for my life. I am sending you a fragment of my helplessness.* He's hunting for his depression." "I used to have a patient," Doktor A. was digressing, "a camp survivor who lost his wife, his second wife, actually, because his entire first family perished in the War. And all of a sudden this old man was visited by the past. Worse, attacked by the past. When his children wanted him to move in with them, into excellent conditions by the way, he started imagining they were taking him back to the camp. 'Herr Doktor, please help me …' I saw him several times a week and I said: 'I'm your student, teach me history, tell me everything, everything you still remember, what comes back to you out of the darkness.

Please be my teacher, my tutor, my mentor.' It seemed to me that he'd accepted the role, he spent a few days telling me about his experiences, studying me closely. Then one day he went silent. We were quiet for almost an hour and then he said to me: 'You're cured. I can do no more.' He even smiled. After a while he added: 'Can we predict the past?' A week later he died."

Doktor A.'s daughter called. "Yes, sweetie, you can buy the T-shirt, the first one, the pink one ... Me too ... You looked very nice in it, we could've bought it straight away ... I'll be late tonight ... Sleep well, bye, darling." He turned back to me. "Great wine, eh? Bought it specially for tonight, Argentinean! Cabernet Sauvignon Oak Cask 2002 from the Mendoza province." "How are you coping?" I asked A, who for the past few years had been the single father of two children: Joanne, now sixteen, and eleven-year-old Adam. His exotic wife had left him for a young German businessman. "Li's phoning more often than usual these days, but just to tell me her life's like a cage closing in on her. And me? I fancy falling in love one more time, but completely, to the bottom, to the utmost neuron. So far it's just routine flings. For the sake of hygiene. You meet a sweet girl, you think maybe she's the one, and suddenly it turns out her backhand's so strong that you drop your racket."

A few months later, Doktor A. from Buenos Aires airport:

"*Buenos días, amigo*, we're at the *aeropuerto*. The girl from my dreams just went past! Brunette, blue-eyed. She's left her blue eyes in mine, and now I'm gazing at this country through her eyes, and I'm in love."
"Hang onto those eyes for the rest of your journey," I say, "Fingers crossed."

That afternoon, a patient to me:

"You know, Herr Doktor, I'm thinking about joining a choir. I once went to a Wagner concert and through my opera glasses I studied the singers' mouths. One second they were opening wide, next second they were closing slightly, twisting out melodic breath."

Pani Róża, to me:

"I've paid for a mass. The priest in Rennweg's going to give it, for my dead granny's soul. But you know what he said to me? 'Roses smell lovely, Pani Róża,' and he'd like a sniff. Is a priest supposed to talk like that?"

My aunt, in my dream: "Don't count on me popping up in your dream."

Susanne, on the phone:

"*Shabriri, Briri, Iri, Ri*, where are you?"

"*Shabriri, Briri, Iri, Ri*, I'm going to the Polish book-shop in Burggasse."

"Can you meet me and talk about demons?" asks Susanne.

"Of course. Herrenhof coffeehouse in an hour, don't mistake me for Robert Musil."

"I'll try not to."

⟳ Z., at the bookshop, to me:

"Herr Doktor, you haven't been in for a while, have you stopped your Polish lessons?"

"I never started," I said. "But I have begun talking Polish with some friends. I've a problem with information processing, I'm held back by my subjective approach to objective matters."

"Then can I offer you a coffee?"

"Delighted."

Z. disappeared up the spiral staircase, and I leafed through some German translations of Polish books.

"I really feel part of your expedition to Poland, and I'm expecting a frank report on your return."

I put down Gombrowicz's *Diary*. I kept thinking about the author's stay in Argentina. He'd set sail just before World War II broke out. Z. poured the coffee into black mugs, looked at me wryly with a mysterious smile. Finally, she said:

"Fantastic."

To which I said:

"Yes, my dear, I'll be crossing a symbolic border in my courageous car. On my left, my unruly imagination can see grass burning like fireworks — I've already heard the stories — on my right, little rusty towns. And a few other topographical generalizations. What else should I know?"

"Well, obviously something about those topographical generalizations. I understand it'll be September, October. Do you have to drive?"

"I don't have to, but I think I will, it'll give me a degree of independence. I just read in the papers that the railways are going on strike, it might be the pilots tomorrow."

"It can happen. Have you booked the hotel yet? I hope they're not going on strike too."

"People have recommended the Hotel France."

"Fantastic, but I've got something better for you, the Park Hotel right next door. My friends have tested it."

"Fantastic," I said, "What's the address?"

I looked at her intensely black dress. It was bright and cheerful somehow.

"You know, I feel as if I'm going to my own wedding without even knowing where my fiancé lives. Or who she is."

"But you've heard quite a bit about her infidelity," Z. laughed.

"All I can count on in this situation are my own weaknesses."

"Have you got any?"

At that moment I saw my aunt enter the bookshop. She turned out to be an Austrian translator of Polish literature. We exchanged a few pleasantries, I bought a German-language guide to Kraków, and on my way out I promised Z. that when I returned I'd employ all my talents to describe my Polish expedition. Then I went to the Herrenhof, buying one yellow tulip on the way. In a short red jacket adorned with black buttons, Susanne was sipping Viennese coffee already.

"A touch of spring," I said about the tulip, "It might cheer you up."

The waiter placed it in a slim carafe.

"What's happened?"

"I think we split up."

"You think? Do you still say hello in the street?"

"I'm serious. We had a heavy conversation."

"Do you still gaze into each other's eyes? No. Do you dream about growing old together? No. He left you long ago, you never even noticed."

"I know now. He was running away from me for

ages but he didn't have the courage to mention it. Not till yesterday."

"Finally. Luckily you're not as wounded as you look. Take a bird's-eye view of yourself. Young, pretty…"

Susanne tried to smile, but soon she was depressed again. The tulip, the witness to our conversation, unfolded its yellow ears as if trying to take in every word. There was an odd couple at the next table. She — a brunette slightly past her sell-by date, with the profile of a bird — with an elegant grey suit, a large ring on her finger, and a low, husky voice. He much younger, blond hair, blue eyes, a navy blue scarf round his neck with large white dots. He looked just off the golf course. He stared into her voice, a little confused and trepidacious. We drank a few more glasses of Veltliner, trying to find the right diagnosis for the love disease, and finally I said: "Take some time off, go with a girlfriend to a nice hot country."

At which point Doktor A. phoned: "We're in Buenos Aires, at the Tortoni restaurant. Pity you're not here, it's wonderful. We're eating *bife de lomo* and listening to *La Cumparsita*. I'm on the track of our business and, whatever happens, I'll come back to Vienna in the eyes of the airport girl."

Me, to Susanne: "You won't be hanging on to this love for much longer, I think. It had to end. Oh, don't forget our little yellow eavesdropper."

I removed the tulip from the carafe, the waiter handed me a serviette.

That evening I gave her a check-up call: "Okay, how are you doing?" "I'm with a girlfriend." I breathed with relief. Probably by tomorrow her endorphins, adrenaline's kin, will be up.

⌒ "God's only excuse," I used to repeat after Stendhal during youthful attacks of heresy, "is that he doesn't exist." During my juvenile protests I wondered what God was like and where he was when he wasn't there. I borrowed words from my reading to describe him. I saw him backed by an abyss sometimes, or in a garden surrounded by close-cropped hedges, in music, especially choral, in the mysteries that my aunt passed on to me, or in the nocturnal expression of the darkness. Then I waited for a sign from the dead on the Other Side, but they gave me none. "He who spoke the world into being" became my familiar Absence. I could have had coffee with him in a nice Viennese café that, according to my aunt, must already be doing great business as a Garden of Eden.

〰   Doktor A. always used to say: "I'm telling you, the only thing that counts is love — love to the end of death. You're lying on a beach, caressing her hair ..." He was always falling bombastically in love, I liked to listen attentively to his spontaneous outpourings. When he came back from Greece he invited me to a meal he cooked himself, a gorgeous moussaka. I watched him chop up the greens, garlic, onions, heat up the oil in the pan, fry the meat lightly, add tomatoes, stew it for a few minutes. I observed with growing admiration as he peeled the potatoes, prepared the sauce, sprinkled cheese over the grand stuff, and popped it in the oven to bake. We sipped ouzo, strong aniseed vodka. I admired A.'s energy, his enthusiasm for life, his optimism. I envied him the qualities I was lacking myself. That's why I was looking forward so much to his return from Argentina. At work he behaved the same way.

I remember one of our first patients, a young writer who published his first book at the age of fourteen. His parents were proud, the critics enthusiastic. He devoted his whole youth to writing. He was a perfectionist, filling lined notebooks with thick, slightly oblique print. As he approached his twenties he entered a self-idealizing phase: "I'm great, but I am unappreciated." He develops neurotic ambition, so common in artists. Success is the measure of perfection, so it's success at any price. I'm almost at the top, but somebody's treacherously cutting the rope I'm climbing. Art's not sport, it can't test itself in competitions — I finished first, that proves I'm best. Our writer published a few more books, but they didn't excite the critics any longer. He went to study in America, where he committed suicide. Doktor A. could not get over this. I remember our discussions, whether it could've been prevented. What seemed so easy in our student years was becoming more and more complicated, like the infinite — and for me always disquieting — number *pi*, the mathematical thriller. In those student years A. often used to pop over, stay for dinner, have discussions with my father. He had lost his own father when he was young, and he grew up surrounded by women, his mother and two sisters. My aunt, whom he wooed at every opportunity, liked him a lot and used to say about him: "A lunatic, but the filling's tasty."

⌒   Doktor A. to me, two days after returning from Argentina: "Look into my eyes, can you see her?" "I can." "Beautiful?" "Beautiful." "I keep thinking about her, I could feel her presence at the airport as we took off to Vienna. Even Joanna suddenly called out, pulling at my sleeve: 'Look, daddy, I think she's running over there!' But it wasn't her, the children were playing tricks on me." My aunt: "He'd best fall in love with a work of art, a still life would be safest."

Doktor A.: "About your mysterious prose: my relatives probably knew the author. He was well-known, an eccentric, he lived in Esmeralda Street. After the War he worked for a few people in Vienna, maybe also for your father, but — just as I suspected — he was also going it alone. He was known to write in Polish and German. He was even published in a Polish émigré paper. And one time he did go to Poland, to a small town, probably in the south. Apparently he was looking for someone too. Looking for someone all the time."
"*Everybody saw it drive through the town, then turn towards the forest.... It drove itself, and it looked like a hearse ..*"
Doktor A.: "It was his escape, this never-ending search. He was running away from the past. My relatives don't know when he died, but they rule out suicide. I suspect he himself condemned his alter ego to death ... We

probably won't solve this mystery. It might still be possible to find the small town in Poland where he went, but perhaps one shouldn't try and solve everything completely?" "Perhaps ..." Doktor A.: "Well, and now about love: Argentina's my type — slim, sensuous, charming, with a touch of the brutal." "I can see it in your eyes," I said.

I put the Argentine mystery away with the other files. All that was left was a tough-to-decipher fragment of somebody's life. And a blurred photograph of my father inserted into an illegible paragraph.

"Pani Róża, I'm going to Poland for two weeks."

"Oh dear!" Pani Róża, who was working with steady movements, suddenly froze. She put her pink cloth in the bucket and repeated:

"Oh dear! What for?" And added a moment later: "Sorry to be asking."

"No problem, Pani Róża, here's my answer. I'm going to do some sightseeing in Kraków."

"It's our Pope's city, I sometimes went there on school trips, lovely churches," Pani Róża said proudly.

"Well, you know, I'd like to see it."

"Really?"

Pani Róża didn't believe my words.

"Really. What else would you advise me to see?"

"I don't know really."

Pani Róża scrubbed at the window sill. I looked at her swathed in the afternoon sun that was lighting a fire.

⌒ I associated packing with navigation: I had to redefine myself in relation to the suitcase lying in front of me. Which port are we sailing to, for how many days, what kind of weather can we expect, and where are we placed — my suitcase and me — on the map of a universe in transit. In life I was guided by the principle of taking as few things as possible; after all, you could buy everything nowadays. But I was a navigator who liked to take books on board, and even — recklessly — fragments of unfinished work.

I've never managed to work while travelling, but the thought that it's possible never abandoned me. On bright slips of paper I wrote down the most important things I must remember to take: a phone charger, a camera, my most accommodating Ecco shoes, my address book, Father's notes, my favourite Gucci: a note of ginger, white pepper, and cinnamon. I could hear my aunt's constant reminders: "The striped shirt doesn't go with your suit, the tie's too showy, take your dressing gown just in case, two pyjamas, felt slippers, two scarves, the German-Polish dictionary, woolly socks, Balsam of Jerusalem." I knew I was going on a "business" trip, though I didn't quite know what it meant. I wanted finally to get to know a fragment of my father's life, while at the same time I was curious about that other world, which overlaid yet another one. Canvas upon canvas. Perhaps I can still discover some rusty threads of linen, the irregular knots, the complicated warp, of time past? Or maybe something similar will happen to what happened in the Czech Republic, when I went with Father to Prague? There in that city I found a universalized new world. The same shops, similar looking young people, the same laughter, the same imitation crocodile handbags. Afterwards I often visited Moravia: Brno and lovely Olomouc, where I was amazed by the remnants of a past that was preserved in carefully refurbished monuments and in the shouts of my friend Vlašek: "They've returned my family's properties! You can move in with me now!" He had a good share of Hrabal's sense of humour, the melancholic tenderness, but at the same time he would stick to his pragmatic, substantial positions in any argument.

The countries that I've visited constitute fragments of a novel called *The European Union*. A multi-narrative novel, even an anti-novel, maybe. I came across scraps that were historical, political, and psychological, but picaresque and squalid. In England I always felt locked in a horror story, in a medieval Gothic castle with heavy-laden storm clouds hanging overhead. In France the laughing adolescent girls, the innocent romantic episodes, the running about on a sandy beach at Trouville, always made me think of Proust and Monet.

Does anything in our life run according to the timetable? I know that, crossing the Austrian-Czech border, I'll stop in the little town Gaweinstal and visit Herr und Frau Rittner to buy a few bottles of the Zweigelt and Grüner Veltliner. We'll chat for a while about this year's harvest and the days getting shorter, and Frau Rittner as usual will say, "Hope it doesn't get any worse," and then, "To the Czech Republic again, Herr Doktor?" But this time I shall say: "To Poland." Outside, the same old dog tries to produce a sound like barking. Whatever happened to the young dogs of our childhood, tearing from fence to fence, furious, uncompromising, confident... I know I'll rest my eyes on cornfields of metal windmills, grinding the air and chasing the birds away. I'll drive past Mistelbach, the great museum of dolls, which you see all over the place: in shop windows, in the windows of people's homes, in cafés. A crowd of porcelain people smelling of fresh coffee. I'll probably stop at a shop between Drasenhofen and Mikulovo, in a no-man's-land between borders that don't exist anymore, although they do. As usual I shall buy mineral water, marshmallows, a bottle of whiskey, and maybe some Fernet Branca, bitter herb vodka, not unlike stomach drops, made from a recipe that's secret still. "*Na shledanou!*" the cashier will say to me. I'll enter the gentle landscape of Moravia, which in autumn looks as if somebody's strewn the roadside with the covers of *Gardens Illustrated*, and at the nearest petrol station I shall have two grilled sausages with mustard and two slices of bread. "Protects us from the heat, the cold, and the harmful demons. Sometimes helps win legal cases." That's what my aunt always said about bread.

⌒ "*He fell upon the little town, sudden as sin ...*" The reception area at the Park Hotel, Kraków. With its odour of transience, so typical of every hotel in the world. A polite young man handed me a registration form to fill out. In the hall was a porter, seven feet tall,

conceivably a retired policeman, dressed up in a uniform
at least two sizes too small. I was always amused by the
liveries of hotel staff, firemen, lodges and brotherhoods,
not to mention cassocks and habits. The combination
of thin wool and gabardine, the grey shades of crepe,
the epaulettes, gold braid and ribbons. As an element of
psychotherapy, I've always associated the Uniform with
the acceptance of significance, difference, with a discov-
ery of "oneself" and "being somebody," and — lurking
behind — with a dangerous line: cross it in extreme
situations and the consequences are usually grim. The
porter studied me carefully, no doubt assessing my status.
Here he was probably misled by my suitcase, a leather
Rolls-Royce designed by Louis Vuitton, which my father
was given as a present many years ago by an Italian
friend. The porter bore the Rolls-Royce reverently into
the lift, and we rose to the second floor. He accepted a
Euro with dignity and gloomily said, "Have a good time
in Kraków." "Thank you." The hotel was in the dark
green range, a large walnut clock in the hall recalled our
family clock. The hands never seemed to move, but the
time was usually right; I found that hard to understand.
It took me a week to realize time was playing with me
in Kraków. The hands teased me, and the maid — who
could have been Pani Róża's double — seduced me with

white sheets, green towels, banal scented soaps, little bottles of shampoo and body lotion.

No doubt my aunt, Doktor Benek, his wife, and cousin Margot would all agree I had chosen the right hotel. It fitted me as snugly as the suit I'd bought at Tlapa's in Favoritenstrasse, where two assistants and a tailor pored over my trouser legs, sticking in tiny pins that they held in their mouths. It was a mystery to me how many pins they could fit between their lips, especially since they were simultaneously mumbling a string of compliments about my build and the quality of the wool the suit was made of. Without, of course, any dubious chemical ingredients, wool substitutes, or synthetics. One of the assistants tugged at my jacket, which was too wide in the shoulders and too short in the sleeves. He finally delivered a lecture about the ideal length of arms, which was hardly in line with Albrecht Dürer's *Four Books on Human Proportions*, and, resigned, he went to fetch another size. The new jacket was a perfect fit, the assistant looked at my reflection and told it: "You won't regret this." The tailor was still crawling at my feet, spitting out another portion of pins. Now dressed in the dark navy blue, nearly black, suit, I left the Park Hotel equipped with maps, addresses, notes, phone numbers, and marshmallows.

↶↷ I was absorbed into the city's sticky damp.
At the street corner I stopped by an art gallery. In
the window I saw a huge portrait of Pope John Paul II,
in a style of unintended grotesque realism. Next to it,
several youths with shaven heads unloaded wooden
birds from a yellow mail van. The street was called
St. John's and led to the Old Town's Market Square.
But I only had eyes for the uneven pavement, protrud-
ing flagstones, jagged curbs, holes in the road, and gaps
in the tarmac. I had to change my walking technique
yet even so almost ended up at the feet of a portly
nun, who had just emerged from a church nearby:
"Oh Jesus," she called, catching me by the hand. My
right eye (the left one was busy with the pavement)
noticed a tea shop on the way, a Rosenthal shop selling
porcelain rabbits, an Irish Pub (symbol of Polish-Irish
friendship), the window of an antique shop with an old
porcelain vase containing a bouquet of black walking
sticks decorated with silver handles of varied shapes
and patterns. In the Market Square I was passed by a
jolly group of English tourists in T-shirts, though the
weather was autumnal and cool. They seemed to have
just quit the warm island of the hotel sauna, and they
still wore the damp warmth of their abandoned sexual
partners. In front of the Sukiennice Cloth Hall there

were *droshky*s waiting; the horses looked heavy and tired, the falling dusk was pierced by camera flashes, a child was clapping, a rustle of pigeons took flight. In the grey corduroy sky the moon rose — Vienna's or Kraków's? I gazed nostalgically into this round Thing, which in my mind belonged purely to me and had even travelled with me to the unknown city. A drunk leafed helplessly through his pockets in search of one last scrap of hope.

I walked to Sarego Street, peeping at the map and the address written down long ago by my father and confirmed by a Pani Maria, who had answered the phone. "You are — ?" A low female voice.

In a situation like this it's best to say: "I am an Austrian writer, I'm writing a novel about a family who stopped in Kraków on their way from Lvov to Vienna." But my father never did live in Kraków. It was just that a friend, somebody close to his heart, had moved here. Sometimes he returned to her absence. Only near the end of his life did he write down the name and address for me: "Mira Wilner, Sarego 11." Obviously, nothing's going to match anymore; neither the name nor the colour of the house, nor the smell of the scullery staircase, nor the scattered props. The details will mist over like glasses that suddenly, carelessly, enter a warm house straight from the rain.

Sarego Street didn't stand out in any way. I was passed by two drunk soldiers. One picks on the other one: "Whatdja want, *kurwa*?" I have to say, the word that I heard most frequently in Kraków, *kurwa* ("whore," literally), was used by all kinds of people: old, young, children, sober, drunk, businessmen, students, priests. It was a comma, a decisive factor in every conversation, sometimes the knockout punch, an expression of love, and a curse.

The door was opened by a slim, brown-haired woman, thirty-something, in jeans and a white blouse. Coloured buttons. The large room, packed with picturesque bric-a-brac, smelled of coffee. A birch desk with the original fittings, probably early twentieth-century, loaded with piles of books. Next to the desk were a Biedermeier gondola chair for a dressing table (totally at odds with the decor), a chest with four drawers, a sofa in need of refurbishment, an eclectic pair of black armchairs, and a dinner table (with four stylized lion's paws) bearing some electronic gadgets, a computer, and two empty cups probably placed there in preparation for our encounter. Next to the books, papers, and newspapers were two felt hats. Above that, a halo of light flooding down from a majolica lamp on the desk. Nothing matched anything else but at the same time constituted a whimsical whole. Maria watched me, amused:

"This room's my granny's restaurant car, that's what she called it. She was always on the move in it. Coffee?"

"With pleasure."

Some rose-jam cakes materialized on the table, exceptionally tasty it turned out. When Maria went briefly to the kitchen I saw my aunt for a moment, sitting on the sofa, contentedly powdering both her nose and my presence in this space that had ceased to exist so long ago.

"You're Austrian," Maria said, more to herself than to me.

I agreed without much conviction, because what does that mean, to be Austrian? Every footballer who can score for Rapid Vienna or SV Salzburg can become an Austrian in a second, even if he's from Brazil. Personally I felt a citizen of the world and a cosmopolitan, which drove my aunt crazy: "Perhaps one day you'll get a divorce from ideas like that."

"Why did your father never telephone my grand-mother?"

"I don't know. I can't explain it."

"Memory gets covered with ivy," my father sometimes said. He never talked to me about love, at times
he even seemed cold and austere, though I remember
one moment when we waited at the bus stop for the 13A
and a girl of unusual beauty stood next to us. She could
have been twelve. We couldn't take our eyes off her and
were probably both wishing for the bus to come late.
But for once the bus was on time and fate was kind,
because the girl got on with us. So in the almost empty
bus we sat opposite a youthful Madonna — sketched by
Cranach or Dürer — who must have escaped from the
Museum of Fine Arts for a moment and decided to try
out riding on buses. What was my father thinking then,
his eyes fixed on a tempting altar of beauty? I hadn't
the courage to ask. We got off with her, or was it only
with the memory of her, at the stop in Neubaugasse.
The street that awaited us was quite empty.

⌒　Maria liked to talk about her life. She was an
art historian and worked at the Museum of History.
"I paint a bit." She was brought up by her grandmother,
her parents died in a car crash. A few years ago she
divorced her husband, a prominent Kraków painter.

She pampered me with florid tales and a certain wilful sense of distance. "Do you have any photographs of your grandmother?" Maria produced a faded album, which reminded me of some passages in the letter from "my" Argentinean, in the *Echoes of a Journey: "Is it right to become an accomplice to somebody's life?"* Dim sepia, the photographs still glowed. The captions were blurred and illegible. 1928 — a group of young people at a lake, yellowing bulrushes, telegraph poles, with heavy rainclouds in the background. 1928 — the uncertainty of young girls, with the calligraphy of the forest in the background. 1926 — a boat with water still flowing through its wooden veins. 1929 — somebody's child amazed by the camera's persistence. 1929 — a road leading to nowhere, shadowless. 1926 — a young woman, next to her a youth in a sports shirt, airtight space between them. 1927 — the same couple on skis. His arm's around her now. The rusted snow, the corroded caption: "Lvov." "Here's my granny, and that's her ski coach." "The ski coach is my father."

Maria: "Hmm. It must have been a pretty good romance."

We leaned over the musty-smelling paper, which for me mingled with the intense fragrance of her chestnut hair. Yes, and Father was a pretty good skier.

He often took us to St. Anton, Kitzbühel, Obertauern, or Lech am Arlberg. The wind would push gently as we schussed down the slope. It must have been a pretty great romance, I thought, swathed in mystery and silence. We shut the album and emerged from the photographs like a pair of tourists lost in time. Maria made some more coffee.

"What are your plans?" she asked me. "I've got no plans. I've only got a few more addresses, which I may try out, though I don't have to ..." "Would you like to see the town and some people who are worth seeing? If you do, I can be your guide."

We began with the Jewish cemetery in Miodowa Street, where Mira is buried. I placed a stone on her grave. It had lain on my father's desk: hard, coarse-grained, porous. The cemetery was deadly tired, stupefied, doubly deceased. Apart from us there was no one there. Maria: "Everybody got dispersed somewhere." Dried-up time, withered. Nearby, the busy road, cars passing, a shopping centre. Life.

⌒⟍⟍   When I got back to the hotel, Susanne rang: "Which planet are you on now? *Shabriri, Briri, Iri, Ri?*

How's life in Kraków?" "*Shabriri, Briri, Iri, Ri.*" She
was in great spirits. "I've met a nice musician, trombone player, undiscovered genius. When did you last
really listen to Mahler's Third Symphony?" "You sound
like the goddess Euphoria," I said. Susanne reported
the news from the surgery, and I briefly sketched the
beauty of the city I was staying in.

In my room I switched on the TV, revealing some
dodgy characters who spoke with the voice of the cab-
bie who brought me to the hotel: "It's all because of our
geography, mister. Russia on one side, Germany on the
other, and now the EU. It's the new partition of Poland.
The dollar's going down and on top of that there's
Hurricane Emma, the air pressure's falling, we didn't
have a winter because they're messing around with
the climate. And who's doing the messing? You know?"
He looked cautiously in the mirror where my face was
reflected. "Nine fifty," he said when we stopped in front
of the hotel. But there were also some more lyrical
cabbies who talked about women as if they were boxes
of chocolates; they were like my patients, awaiting their
moment, awaiting their chance to throw themselves
into a whirl of words and the brute force of meanings.

I had problems with sleep. I could hear raised
French voices through the wall. I switched the light

on and started reading *Cognitive Therapy*, by Judith
S. Beck, whom I'd met in America at Pennsylvania
University. A recitation through the wall:

> *La sécheresse dans ma tête est si grande*
> *que je dois prendre garde*
> *de ne pas mettre le feu*
> *à la mémoire.*

And again, a moment later:

> *La sécheresse dans ma tête est si grande*
> *que je dois prendre garde*
> *de ne pas mettre le feu*
> *à la mémoire.*

Then a short sigh: "*Oh, mon Dieu, oh, mon Dieu…*"
Silence. But silence refined, reconciled. I was
falling asleep in someone else's one-act play, in a very
snug double bed. A dream sent me recklessly back
to the album. Now the photographs all showed us
together, Maria and me. Even the year 1926 dissolved,
in unexplained circumstances.

Doktor A. texted me at breakfast: "How is it going?
Am chased by facts as usual. Dr. Benek asked about

you, Susanne's in love." I went for a short walk. I like the morning buzz, the cracks of a day not yet quite woken, the smell of coffee married to a daily paper: in Kraków that wasn't so easy, the few cafés that opened at eight faced the obvious opposition of the waiters. There was also a lack of foreign papers. The aromas were usually restricted to toasted cheese and mushroom sandwiches. Kebabs featured a lot, too, wrapped in noisy exotic music. I noticed the vans delivering bread attracted pigeons who strutted proudly all over the fresh loaves and buns, cooing with satisfaction.

The sunrise was beckoning, forecasting a cool but sunny day. Finally, in Krótka Street, which Maria had mentioned, I found the Limerick Café, where I could drink decently prepared hot chocolate and at least cast an eye over a Polish paper. The café was mainly occupied by young people, students, immersed in carefree discussions. Still free from the torment of ambiguity and uncertainty, they burst into laughter at every chance. Looking at them, I marvelled at myself from many years ago, when self-confidence, absolute and unshaken, sat on my lap, guaranteed for life. The velvet-smooth hot chocolate left a sensuous imprint in my mouth. I read in the paper that dozens of exorcists had been appointed by the Polish church, to take care of citizens possessed by the Devil. Expert psychiatrists expressed extreme caution, but the priests stated they had extensive experience in this area, and positive results. In the case of a prisoner from Sieradz, the judge supported the exorcist. "Possession by Satan does not stand up in court," commented a Ministry of Justice spokesman. This news matched a book I saw in a bookshop window, *The Miracles of John Paul II*, who's surely due for beatification sometime soon.

I heard my aunt's voice: "If you swallow a snake, eat a bag of salt, then run three miles."

I arranged to meet Maria for lunch. "At the Louvre," she said, "the French restaurant in Krótka Street." I was finding myself in Krótka Street more and more often, but I didn't give up on the other districts. With the help of Maria and coincidence, I discovered new chapters of the city unforeseen in any tourist guide. "You know, in this town my life works like a self-propelling machine," I told Maria, "the *perpetuum mobile*." We called each other by our first names now, having drunk a toast with an excellent red wine from Upper Galilee, specially recommended by the *chef de la maison*, who was something of a character. The waitress lit our candle, and then in Maria's honey eyes I saw the year 1929, two bonfires and a group of laughing students. Increasingly I realized that there is no place for the past tense outside of grammar. My past kept changing places with future facts and events, spreading through me like a virus. The present trickled out from the desserts, especially the lemon tart they served here, and then ran away. In Kraków Maria, the accomplice of my present tense, did all she could to help it abscond. The passing hours lost their meaning for me, I felt I was a one-man expedition cared for by a sherpa who was laying on charming social trips, guided tours, visits to hospitable friends.

⌒ I loved roaming aimlessly round the town with Maria. We strolled into bars, old neglected parts of town, dingy parks where spilled rubbish frightened the visitors and the greenery seemed wracked with agony. I was amazed by the funeral parlours located opposite hospitals. I imagined a patient staring at the black and silver letters of "Epitaph," "Hearse," "Dahlia," or "Lily." I was quite taken aback by the triviality of it all. The hospital in Dolnych Młynów Street had a firm advertising funeral services on one side and the Groteska Puppet Theatre on the other. Perhaps death does have something grotesque about it, think of Hans Baldung Grien's paintings where Death's drawn to plump young ladies and a merry life. Over my desk in Vienna I've a copy of an Edvard Munch that I bought in Oslo, *Death and the Maiden*, the essence of eroticism, bliss, and terror.

⌒ In Miodowa Street, Maria told me the story of the Tempel Synagogue. She spoke in a hushed voice though we were alone in there, with only the light to eavesdrop, light that sketched tottering shadows, shapes of anxiety, silhouettes of figures, streaks of dates. Maria paused at every detail. Precious murals and stucco decorations breathed back her words. The galleries began to fill up with women. To the right of the *aron ha-kodesz* storing the scrolls of the Torah, the dead cantor appeared. We were extracted from the atmosphere by the piercing sound of a car alarm.

A VW Golf, its lights pulsating, attracted no one's attention though it wailed like a factory siren. We made our way towards the town centre, passing little neglected streets with ruined houses. Refurbished tenements, hotels, restaurants sprang up suddenly between them, each one bedecked with architectural tinsel. On the walls were the odd swastika, Stars of David hanging from the gallows, and inscriptions: "Gas the Jews," "Queers out," "I love people"— signed: "The Cannibal."

A phone call from Benek: "How's it going in Kraków? What's the weather like? Margot wants to know if you've been robbed. It's good you don't understand much about Polish politics; what we watch on TV's not exactly appetizing." The Beneks could get a High-Definition patriotic channel, TV Polonia, and from time to time they told me some grim tales about Low-Definition politics — incompatible with European standards and their advanced equipment.

My aunt: "They should switch on the parental control and finally stop killing themselves." Me to Benek: "I read the papers, I'm up to date, the weather's friendly."

The morning walks I'd steadily grown used to kept taking me to Krótka Street. I made friends with the street, which was not long, but disciplined. Inconspicuous two- and three-storey townhouses, some in urgent need of construction therapy, bore their chronic ailments with great pride. They were the living undead. Every day polyglot crowds poured out from the ground floors of ruined structures. On my way from the hotel to Krótka

Street I'd pass the same familiar addicted faces for whom morning, frustrating in its cool sobriety, was excuse enough to empty another vodka bottle. The hurrying-to-work folk paid them no attention. At the Limerick, the *Bank Gazette* already had a few readers. The main stock exchange indexes had closed with large losses again. It wasn't good news. In Vienna the victims of the index's constant volatility often ended up in our clinic. Some lost their fortunes and their touch with reality. They covered sheets of paper with numbers, diagrams. On their personal stock exchange, shares in loneliness were rising.

From the tower of St Mary's Church a bugle call killed nine o'clock. The waitress smiled at me: "Cappuccino?" Along with the coffee, which steamed with white froth sprinkled with chocolate gravel, she served me a morning paper.

"Do you think I'll understand it all?"

"It's not so difficult."

"Can you understand it all?"

"I don't even try."

It was a sentence sprinkled with bitterness. Without

giving up on her smile, she retreated to the kitchen.
I could ask myself the same question: Do I understand
it all, why my father shunned the one fragment of his
past that still glowed with the faint, dim light of a
lantern on a grave? Someone's sorrow was still fawn-
ing over those dates. A call from Maria: "How'd you
sleep?" "Like a tourist." "Oh, recreational sleep. We've
an invite to a birthday banquet — S. She's a barrister.
You'll come and pick me up around eight?" I was allot-
ted the task of purchasing flowers and Lindt chocolates.
As I left the Limerick, the grimaces of the Sukiennice
Cloth Hall gargoyles pierced the mist.

␥   First I was aware of dark brown hair — tea
and rum; eyes — honeydew, which reflected a coronet
of guests; a smile — warm and inviting; a voice — *violi
d'amore* flavoured with the whiskey that Barrister S.
was holding in her hand. "At last! Wonderful! Maria's
told me lots about you, you must make yourself at
home." For the next fifteen minutes Maria kept intro-
ducing me relentlessly —"Dr. Sefer, from Austria"—
followed by the surnames of the persons I was meeting
and sometimes their honourable professions: "Chief

of the Court of Appeal," "Chief of the Administrative Tribunal," "Vice-Chief of the High Court." But just as I was approaching the Lord Chief Justice of the Last Judgment, I encountered some artists, entertainers, academics, doctors.

I looked at Maria proudly. In a little black dress with a touch of extravagance, she looked wonderful. When she dedicated me a knowing glance, something flickered inside and for the first time I felt some mutual, intangible understanding between us. Maria was known and popular in this hospitable house, she dished out kisses and hugs. Her female friends and acquaintances looked at me hungrily: "Ah, you're the one." I bowed over their well-groomed hands and, in accordance with Austrian custom, skimmed the fragrances — cinnamon, jasmine — hovering above them. After an hour and a certain quantity of desirable drinks, I was already part of a sociable team, scoring in discussions and winning sympathizers and fans.

I must mention that I can't recall when I last encountered such a delicious menu. There simply aren't enough panegyrical adjectives — the sophisticated vegetable salads, herrings, stuffed goose necks, soured gherkins, mushrooms, borscht, not to mention the monumental gâteaux and desserts that broke divine interdictions. I could hear my overjoyed aunt: "Beetroot broth's so kind to the heart and so good for the eyes."

A cabaret star, poetically drunk: "I'm the bard of our time, you know." He skipped the formal "*Pan*" and addressed me familiarly. "Let me tell you about all these people. Take that artist and his beautiful wife — she's too beautiful for him to be a decent painter — or take this country, though it doesn't have a beautiful wife. It should be an EU folk museum, the Communist Ethnographic Heritage Centre. We could go back to brewing moonshine, restore the underground press. Vodka, cigarettes, toilet paper, ration the lot! We'll publish Lenin's works, and the sanatoria that the Secret Police used to run can give spa treatments to Western tourists. Obviously, we'd need to be financed by the EU because, my friend, we can't cope with freedom." The bard suddenly floated away and I found myself in a cluster of music lovers: "I'm especially attuned to the expression of the Romantics. When I listen to the songs of Schubert, or Schumann, or Mendelssohn, I'm like a lunatic in a world rendered unreal." I had the chance to meet a great music expert, Barrister R.

"This fugue is permutational." He meant Bach's Mass in B Minor. "Can you hear the second soprano?" There was also talk, or rather a monologue, about the harmony of thirds, the implacable necessity of the bass, Gregorian chants, *Et in unum Dominum*, and about the phenomenon of musical meditation. I was fascinated by his erudition, his joyous enthusiasm.

"Oh, Professor, do you remember my MA exam?" A certain lady of an inscrutable age asked a famous — I later was to discover — retired theoretician of literature. "Professor, you failed me." "I remember, madam." "You've made me remember, for the rest of my life, that Reymont's *Promised Land* was published in 1896." "You are mistaken, madam, *The Promised Land* came out in 1899. 1896 was *The Comedienne*." Nearby there was a political conversation: "The president's still out to cause trouble."

Just a few days after my arrival I started hearing tasty political anecdotes, though I couldn't get them all. Politicians have never attracted my attention. "Look at that corrupt, insolent pink poodle," my aunt used to say, aiming her index finger at the TV screen. Although it seemed to be, Poland certainly was no exception here.

I liked the looks of a lady notary public in an amaranth suit: "Everything you say to me, doctor, may have legal consequences." "If we draw up a deed, madam …" I started shyly. The ladies' laughter set in motion the agates, sapphires, aquamarines, amethysts, and rubies around their necks. I absorbed harmonies of elegance, colours, fragrances, and shapes. Maria, standing across the room from me, had for some time been ringed by a pack of young smooth-haired hounds, and one of them, very dark hair, kept telling her something that evidently pleased her. Gently leaning on the window sill, she looked relaxed. Was I jealous?

At that point an older, well-groomed lady approached me: "I knew your father. From the Lvov days. I used to go skiing with Mira, Maria's grandmother." "I never had a chance to meet Pani Mira." "She was very ill." "What kind of skier was my father?" I asked. "An amusing one. How long are you in Kraków?" "I leave in a few days." "I won't ask when you'll be back, I'm not here very often myself, but I'm glad I could meet you. Do you ski?" "Not as amusingly as my father, I'm sure."

A moment later I was introduced to a silent poet who moved through room after room as if it were Ghost Town. We exchanged visiting cards, I learnt he was born in Austria. His esoteric sensitivity didn't seem human. My eyes made notes on several other of the evening's chapters. A vast bouquet of laconically beautiful dark red roses was carried in. It said "I love you" with mathematical exactness. Late guests were still arriving, others left. I watched as Barrister S., like a sensitive traffic policewoman, handed out friendly signals.

I wanted to frame the party with that other time: 1928 — a group of young people at a lake, yellowing bulrushes, telegraph poles, with heavy rainclouds in the background. 1928 — the uncertainty of young girls, with the calligraphy of the forest in the background. 1926 — a boat with water still flowing through its wooden veins. 1929 — somebody's child amazed by the camera's persistence. 1929 — a road leading to nowhere, shadowless. 1926 — a young woman, next to her a youth in a sports shirt, airtight space between them.

Maria jolted me out of my reverie. "Do you know what time it is?" "I do".

⌒⌐ Leaving Barrister S., we were startled by the emotionless night, and by a marked chill. "How about a grappa?" I asked Maria, slowly doing up the buttons of her coat and prolonging the game under the pale street-light. "How about a grappa?" I repeated the question. Maria: "Why not?" And we landed in a psychotropic bar, The Extremist. When we'd made ourselves comfortable in a corner and ordered some drinks, we had a friendly gossip about the highly admirable banquet.

"You've just been in the Other Poland." Maria said.

"And where's the first one?"

"Everywhere else! Whenever I go away, the only people I ever miss are the people you've just met. And those you won't have time to meet."

"And don't you miss the city?" I asked.

"It's beautiful at five in the morning, when it's empty…" Maria said.

Her femininity was gently nudging my imagination, but at the same time kept pushing me towards the pictures her photographer friend was enlarging for me. The world wasn't made for our love, I think. We weren't its type.

⌒⌐   The first symptoms of History appeared during a meeting at Club 68, where Maria and I went, encouraged by a journalist friend of hers. This was an evening with a priest, a Catholic University professor and historian who had written some popular books. Unfortunately, owing to traffic jams, which Maria called "rush hour migraines," we missed everything except the closing questions. The room was red hot. They were discussing the difficult Polish-Jewish relations, though my impression was they were only discussing Polish-Polish relations. "There's constant talk about Polish Jews or Jewish Poles —" A voice from the floor: "Is that good or bad?" A plump lady, looking like an art deco chandelier with a storm of crystal hair and narrow candlestick nose: "But I'd like to know who's behind it all. Well? Who?" She shook her coloured crystal off her forehead. "We're leaving," I said to Maria. Outside, a flickering billboard: "You can win the war against dandruff."

⟋⟍ Breakfast at the hotel, a conversation with a waiter. The same one for ten days. Slight, slim, pale, with slightly shaking damp hands. Red eyes, clearly short of sleep but not because of women. I know patients like this, armed with a games console, buried in the trench of his room or in temptation-packed arcades. I could imagine him in a room in a pre-war Kraków tenement block, with a lichen-covered staircase and the incurable smell of damp. Perhaps I even sensed that smell at breakfast when he served my soft-boiled egg. I pretended I couldn't hear the plate shake.

He came from a small village near Radom, had five brothers and sisters, a college degree in hotel management and catering, and a plan — like most young people in Poland — to go to Ireland. "Then I'll come back and set up my own hotel," he said, looking in my eyes for confirmation that he could do it. "I'm sure you can do it." He probably spent his nights on Formula 1 tracks in the Côte d'Azur, amidst the deafening roaring of engines at the Monaco Grand Prix. He was eaten up by his race simulator, the operating system managed his sleepless nights. I imagined him lying in moist excitement, his white shirt clinging to his body, in some rented room with a leaking tap, lying on a metal bed where the landlord's mother may have passed away, for somebody surely must have died on the metal bed one day. He seemed completely saturated with that long-term dying; even the mattress — the lithium-ion battery of the bed — was exhausted and totally used up.

He was thrilled, telling me about the artificial intelligence of the denizens of Liberty City, about the contract killers and his portable console's liquid crystal display. The only thing that was still real in his life was his PlayStation Portable, which took him on a trip into gigabyte solitude nightly. "How do you like it in

Kraków?" he enquired, serving another coffee. "Nice town," I replied.

Doktor A. called to tell me about the results of the brainscan carried out on our patient. We'd suspected the beginnings of Alzheimer's. "It doesn't look too good." And a moment later: "I met a cute blonde. Smells like vegan food." "Bravo!" I said. "Did you meet her on a Lentil Friday?" "At parents' night at Joanna's school." I wasn't giving up: "That's fast." "That's a feast, more like! When will you be back?" "In a couple of days." "I'm looking forward to a meal, with all the details." "Me too," I laughed. "How's Susanne?" "Still mingling with the wind instruments," Doktor A. said. "Thank God." Then Maria called, asking if we might pop into the Limerick, they had a private event that afternoon.

⌒   At the Limerick, the atmosphere was *fin de siècle*. A pale idyll of eccentric boys at the bar, decadent twilight.

"I'm Karolina," a young attractive brunette, the daughter of a famous singer, told me flirtatiously. "And your name's Sefer. And this is my cat, Felix."

"You're absolutely right, my name's Sefer."

"You'll have some wine?"

"With pleasure."

"Red?"

"Do you have green?"

"Of course."

"Then green, please. Semi-sweet."

"We've only sweet."

I liked the girl: intelligent, provocative, confident. The cat — scared and startled — tried to wriggle out of her arms. She passed him on to her obliging valet and a moment later brought two glasses. Mine contained a green mint liqueur.

"Was this your dream?"

"This was my dream."

She told me about the blitzes of artists on the Limerick, about her studying for a teaching degree that bored her to death, about travel. I looked at this child with amazement; her whole body, weighing hardly more than seven stone, seemed to say, "The world's my oyster."

"Mister, I know what you mean."

"I'm sure."

"You could be a poet."

"Oh, I don't think so. It's a job for astronomers."

"Haven't you ever written any poems?"

"Never. Except once. I wrote an island."

"An island?"

"Yes. I invented it and then decided to describe it on sixteen pages. It was exceptionally boring."

"And?"

"What's this conspiracy about?" A young man unceremoniously joined us.

"Herr Doktor Sefer — Alexander, our Artist Laureate."

"I've seen your graphics, in my friend's house."

"And what about this island?" Karolina was looking at me skittishly.

"She got married. He turned out to be a rich, great continent."

"That's my dream, a husband like that." She sighed.

Noisy conversations sucked us in, half-broken words, sentences, shouts, laughter. There was talk about some book that hadn't come out yet but had already been criticized for being too rushed. Where was my story rushing to? I asked myself, looking helplessly round for Karolina, who'd surely answer my question for me.

⌒ I stuck another evening in my Polish collection, another photograph album, another cluster of girls and boys like Stefan Zweig characters setting off to war — in this case war with a restless, neurotic life — and who seemed to be saying: "It'll be over by Christmas." As I was about to leave the Limerick for a moment, just to get some fresh air, Karolina suddenly popped up in front of me. Looking at my empty glass, she said:

"My uncle Shakespeare says empty vessels make the most noise."

"And my aunt Sappho says you can't get everything in life. So you must make choices. And I've already chosen — green tea."

"I understand, everything's green today."

"You understand very well."

She was amusing, intriguing, slightly spoilt, possessive. And again someone snatched her away, and she sent me the dramatic look of a kidnap victim. I hope my paternal smile soothed her romantic anguish. I looked hopelessly for Maria. I was beginning to feel the tiredness and a physical need to change my clothes. My shirt felt uncomfortable, my shoes were pinching me and my tie strangling me. I had problems with my skin. I went outside. I felt the chill, piercing dampness of autumn. I called Maria's mobile. She answered only after a long while.

"Enjoying yourself?" she asked.

"It's great, but I have to go back to the hotel."

"I can walk with you."

I explained to Maria, who'd fled the Limerick hot and flushed, that I still had to call the clinic and talk to Doktor A., who was on duty.

On our way to the hotel Maria and I talked about the double nature of language, which can suddenly flick you from a smart sophisticate into a lout. Just a moment ago language was entertaining us with the brilliance of its wit and palette, only to announce suddenly in the middle of the town square: "I'm *kurwa* trying to explain it to him, and he just gobbles up his fucking sausages!"

Maria went back to rejoin her friends while I phoned Doktor A. at the clinic. He read me part of a letter from a patient whose history he'd tried to build into a case study: *"Dear Herr Doktor, why won't I answer personal questions? Because I never answer personal questions. Do you remember what Goethe wrote about Werther? 'Oh, how often I've cursed those foolish pages that made my youthful torments public property!' We live in an age of collective exhibitionism; we strip ourselves naked mercilessly, down to the bare void. The void that traps us forever. And you, Herr Doktor, think that I'll tell you everything, undress down to the last nerve. You all know too much about me anyway. I bet when I'm wired up for my ECG, you're recording the love inside my heart. Nowadays everything belongs to everybody and nobody.*" Doktor A.: "So I arranged to meet him outside the clinic. And in two hours he told me much more than I would've got on the record." "And how's your vegan blonde?" I asked. "Or is she a kosher brunette now?" "Not yet, but you'd better come back to Vienna soon. I don't like diagnosing over the phone."

⌒ In Kraków I still had a meeting with Barrister R., and I visited the widow of Stanisław Lem. While having coffee with the barrister, I listened fascinated to his thoughts about music.

"Can you believe it, my memory goes back more and more to the sounds of my childhood. Even today a falling object, the sound of breaking glass, it's a plucked note to me. I could sort out the sounds, move them round like wooden blocks, divide them into positive and negative and 'boundary situations,' that's what Jaspers calls them — suffering, death ... Bach. Albinoni. A world of dodecaphonic memories, my nanny's twelve-tone compositions in the kitchen, as she moved the pots and pans. I remember slammed doors ... The sounds varied, you see; depending on the mood and the situation, the doors closed *andante* or *appassionato*, or *fortissimo*. And later," the dreaming barrister went on, "the sounds were joined by hymns in the church. Our devout nanny made us appreciate: this was immortality ... Have you ever sung in the choir?"

"No." I answered weakly. "I probably wasn't a musical child."

"Rubbish. Everyone's musical, they just don't know. The choir enforces discipline. Order. Harmony. Have you ever listened to the Gregorian chants? *Cantus ad Missam ...*"

Without waiting for my answer, he added:

"I remember the wind — gales, storms, horns, metal instruments — when nanny closed the windows and we clung together afraid. Then we'd fall into the abyss of the Fable. For us faith was a metaphysical fairy tale, something between the material world — when we went with nanny to church — and the thing that haunted us inside: the organ, harp, castanets ..."

We went on for a long time talking about Beethoven's Concerto for Violin, Cello, and Piano in C Major, Op. 56 (performed by the Berlin Philharmonic with David Oistrakh, Mstislav Rostropovich, Sviatoslav Richter, conducted by Herbert von Karajan), about Mozart's string quartets, Paganini's concertos... I invited the barrister to Vienna, we exchanged cards.

He asked, "Do you know how many minims we've been talking for? My chambers! I've got to fly."

⌒ A call to Susanne: "*Shabriri, Briri, Iri, Ri.* Happy?"

⌒ Only once in Kraków did I have a chance to go by tram — number 18. To my surprise the tram was built in Austria, with the "Aussteigen" sign still by the door. I went two stops, thinking about immortality. Immortality was linked with my visit to the Lems' and a comment the late writer made about an article in the *International Herald Tribune*. The article posed the question: "What will people die from in a hundred years' time?" Disagreeing with some statements in the article, Lem claimed in his own column that certain human processes are irreversible and "*death, while obliterating the individual specimen, is also the motor of evolution. If there were no death nobody, or strictly speaking nothing, could populate the Earth, except for bacteria.*" Why did his widow and I talk about this at dinner? It was as if we were waiting for him to come and eat while I put off the inevitable truth that he wasn't going to appear on the wooden stairs, as he had in Vienna, and say: "Guess what, I died again the day before yesterday." But we were also recalling the plums (oval and plump, wrapped in velvety skin) that my aunt made *povidel* with, and everybody else who was absent and wasn't covered by the immortality scheme. We were accompanied by the yelling of the Lem dogs: four dachshunds and a Yorkshire terrier that tried to dominate the racket with his falsetto squeak. It felt good in that house, rather like some extra-Krakovian civilization.

We didn't try to predict the future but, trustingly, we arranged to meet again, in Kraków or Vienna.

Now, on tram 18, I was studying three young women talking over each other, loudly, emotionally. One girl's statement overlapped with another's, while the third exploded with laughter. A moment later they swapped roles: the second girl laughed, the third one tossed up a verbal avalanche. I would have trouble describing their appearance: it was the sum of three likenesses. All three of them together constituted one form. An old lady sitting by the window crossed herself elaborately, though it was the photocopier's we were passing. A friend of Maria's had told us how his aunt broke her arm when the tram took a sharp turn by the Franciscan church. At that unfortunate moment she let go of the plastic handle to cross herself. A few weeks in plaster plunged her into depression.

As I watched the three loud girls, I wondered how medicine was going to prolong their lives. Perhaps it would give them a kidney, a heart, or a liver transplant. Or perhaps "the brash pens of American journalists," as Stanisław Lem would have put it, would seduce them with a new mirage, immortality. At that point I had to get off. I said goodbye to my tram, to 18, the number that symbolized life.

⌒ I spent my last days in Kraków on brief walks and talks with Maria. I was sorting out my Kraków landscape by making notes and sipping cappuccino in the Old Town Market Square. I sat in a well-known café, mainly frequented by the average tourist. The young waiters tuned into the average perfectly, with provincial behaviour. They whispered in each other's ears, exchanged knowing looks, and then burst out laughing, nudging one another and drowning the customers' appeals. In the almost empty cloakroom a man stood, silent and non-dimensional. Above the cake cabinet a bee buzzed, trying to cut through the glass, or perhaps only waiting for the moment when the glass curtain would rise.

I observed a woman with ice cream and cherries and caramel cream in front of her in a crystal bowl. She moved her tongue sensuously along a thin spoon, completely, unquenchably immersed in her appetite. For a long time she ignored her ringing mobile phone, which slithered on the table, evidently set on Vibrate. At last, licking her full fleshy lips, she answered. "Hello darling, I'm sitting in our café.... You don't say!" She passed the phone over to her left hand, so as not to interrupt her love affair with the melting ice cream. I opened the paper, from which I learnt that in Poland "Satan works through his agents in the secular press." This was announced by a priest at a solemn mass in Częstochowa. The next news came from London: a chaffinch had learnt to imitate the sound of a telephone and usually did so during banquets when the guests were in the garden. It must have been amused by the sight of the humans racing back indoors to answer the phone. The woman opposite me, loudly: "It's normal, women our age are all long dead." Then she swallowed a cherry, smiling and relaxed. Her last sentence amused me, considering she was about thirty. Then she called the waiter, dropped a crumpled banknote on the table and brusquely left the café. The waiter wiped away all traces of her, firmly polishing the marble surface. A moment later a bizarre couple took the table. He looked like a 1950s' valve radio, with one green, deep-set magic eye; she was a marketing masterpiece by Andy Warhol, with bright rouged cheeks — a tomato soup can. By the time I left they hadn't exchanged a single word. The oddness of the situation lay in the fact that, sitting next to them, I could still see the woman who had just left the café. This was a signal for me, it was time to call the waiter.

In the Market Square I bumped into Karolina. When she saw me, she blushed and said:

"I've bought a new handbag." She waved a neat black box before my eyes. "In a conservative colour."

"You can see straight away it's a baddie," I said casually.

"Isn't it pretty?" Clearly she was anticipating enthusiasm from me.

"Pretty?" I repeated, "Your uncle Shakespeare would write a sonnet about it."

"And your aunt Sappho would compose hymns. Are you still coming to see us?" She put on big sunglasses.

"To say my goodbyes."

"We hate goodbyes."

"That's absurd. I'll see what I can do about it."

⌒○ Maria brought me copies of the photographs: brutally fresh enlarged quotations from the past on Kodak Portra Sepia de luxe paper. As I looked at them I grew more and more bewildered and confounded.

"Don't you like them?" Maria asked, nervous.

How could I tell her that these copies couldn't breathe? This isn't snow, this is a snow effect, a stylization of the past. 1928 — a group of young people at a lake, retouched bulrushes and corrected heavy rainclouds. 1928 — the high-contrast uncertainty of young girls, with the calligraphy of the forest in the background. 1929 — a false road leading to nowhere. 1926 — airtight space overexposed.

"Don't you like them? Would you like the originals?" Maria snatched the photos from my hands and put them in her handbag.

"Give them back," I said without conviction, because in all truth I didn't want them anymore. In my memory I was carrying that old, worn life that still breathed within me.

"I'd like to take you to the Louvre for a farewell dinner," I said.

⌒⌒ My aunt's Talmudic question, "Who shall inherit the future?" remained unanswered. I was watching a motionless figure covered in gold paint posing in Kraków's Market Square: a public meditation amidst the traffic, a hot stew of noisy people all round.

A few months previously, Doktor A. and I had gone to Tel Aviv for a convention at the Medical Center. In the evening I left the hotel for a short walk. It was warm, the wind kept bumping shamelessly into pedestrians. In the bustle of Ben Yehuda Street I saw a woman play-ing the cello. Her knees embraced the soundbox, her eyes followed the bow, but it took me a while to realize these eyes were sightless. The music was deafened by passing buses, the roar of engines, an ambulance in despair, blaring horns, a garrulous fast-food bar. Choosing one of the busiest streets, the woman must have been trying to kill off her unfulfilled life with one Bach suite.

What could connect a woman in Tel Aviv with a motionless golden figure in the Kraków Market Square? A documentary? Fate? My memory?

⌒ "I like it better when you smile," I said to Maria. She was earnestly studying the menu at the Louvre.

"These dishes," she replied, "are deadly serious."

"Then let's have a French anecdote as an entrée. How about frog's legs?"

The Louvre was like a private party, we knew almost everyone there. Across the tables we exchanged comments about art, the films to see, the weather. With her right thumb, Dr. Ola (who did know everyone there), an enthusiast for acupuncture and alternative medicine, was pressing the wrist of a local poetess who suffered from breathing problems. But the restaurant breathed, breathed a conspiratorial air, hinting at mysteries we all begin to understand. In Vienna it would be impossible. Kraków constantly surprised me. Attracted and repelled me at the same time.

"I hope you'll make some medical notes after your trip," Maria said.

"If this country were my patient, I'd have to confine it in my clinic and subject it to intensive analysis."

"But maybe the patient's incurable?" Maria asked.

"I don't think so. One would have to probe down into the deepest levels of history, into disorders on the borders of the subconscious. Let's assume the patient's afraid of the European reality, of freedom, frogs and spiders and everything else. He becomes aggressive —"

"And what would you recommend, Herr Doktor?" Maria was amused. "Drugs and powders? We love those. Especially the powders, like ashes in crypts."

"Not at all. I'd apply cognitive behavioural therapy or hypno-analysis."

"Hypnotize a country?

"Well, when the patient has sporadic irrational impulses combined with an historically grounded fear of the past, hypno-analysis might just do the trick."

"Oh," Maria waved her hand dismissively, "It's so simple for you. You're off back home and that's it. You're leaving us behind like something in a cartoon."

"Come to Vienna."

"To be your cleaner?"

"Oh, not at all, that's Pani Róża's domain. No, I'm serious. Come."

"Maybe, maybe…" she smiled the way I liked. A draught fluttered a chestnut lock on her forehead. Carefully, sadly, she looked at me. To stop the evening from turning into a mawkish sentimental farewell, I asked her shoe size.

"Shoe size?" She laughed.

"I saw some nice autumn shoes at Scholl's next door. Like a look?"

"Colour?"

"Black."

"Pedigree?"

"Clarks."

"Pedigree's not bad. You'd like to buy them for me?" she asked unceremoniously.

"And could I?"

"Provided they look Flemish."

"I'm sure they do."

Suddenly we were approached by Dr. Ola, full of enthusiasm and red wine, asking Maria about the health of some mutual friend. When she learnt I was a medical practitioner, she eyed me with suspicion. But she warmed to me when I told her the story of how my friend A. and I tried biofeedback to influence our body functions, bringing our blood pressure up and down or slowing our heart rate.

"There we lay, all wired up," I narrated it like a thriller, "connected to various gauges, observing our physical parameters on the monitor. We felt we were on a plane flying us into an extraterrestrial reality."

"Anything," Dr. Ola summed up, bidding us a heartfelt goodbye, "is better than chemical poison."

We dissected our trout quietly. "Fish bones," I heard my aunt's voice, "are stumbling blocks."

After a pause I asked Maria: "In Poland, what do you associate with the word 'Jew'?"

"Fox-fur collars and everything that brings bad luck in life. But in Europe now you know, anti-Polonism, if you can call it that, is in fashion. There's an image that's begun to haunt the Poles, and they're finding it hard to escape. If a car's been stolen, it's a Pole; a drunken mother and her kids — that's Poland; muck and cigarette ends thrown out the window, like in my house — it's Poland. And if someone's anti-Polish, obviously he must be a Pole too. It's their religion. Amen." Maria finished, placing her fishbone jewellery on the edge of her plate.

"Do the shoes have laces?" she asked after a while.

"Yes, they have … See you tomorrow at eleven at Scholl's."

We clinked glasses. I said goodbye to the Louvre, hugging friends and total strangers. The uncommon situation made me think of the time in Vienna, in the grounds of the Am Steinhof psychiatric hospital, when I was suddenly approached by a patient who hugged me in spasms of tears, saying, "But you promised! But you promised!" Jokes saw us to the door of the Louvre, laughter barked all round us until we reached the Market Square.

"A blue moon," my aunt used to warn me, "will steal your sleep." The moon wasn't blue, but it was veiled in mist. At the hotel I opened my window wide and breathed in air that smelled of new-mown car fumes. I read two texts on my mobile. One from Susanne: "*Shabriri, Briri, Iri, Ri*, I'm happy." The other was from Karolina: "Me and uncle Shakespeare wish you a midsummer night's dream."

⌒ Next day we bought the Clarks pedigree shoes. Maria immediately brought them to life and asked for the old pair to be wrapped. We also bought an expensive black anti-wrinkle shoe cream. Leaving the shop, we behaved like real tourists. Maria took out her camera, we sat down in an open-air café. The waiters as usual tried to discourage us from ordering coffee, but as my psychiatrist colleagues would say, we were determined and assertive. We hunted for someone who'd take our photograph together. First a few noisy school trips went past, some priests, three girls with kebabs, several students deep in thought, a soldier after a morning drink, a nun, two cyclists. It seemed to me that as they passed us, everyone sped up. In full view on our table top lay a Canon digital camera. Our hunt closed in, a young man walked into the open-air café as if right into our trap. Maria reacted instantly, expertly dragging him into our photo-conspiracy. The man put away his paper, smiled, took hold of the camera and started snapping, becoming incredibly lively and talkative.

"Maybe — against the hydrangea." He kept rearranging us and circling. "Get a bit closer together, right, heads closer, closer ..."

I virtually embraced Maria, our heads stuck together like ivy to a wall. In high spirits, we made our way to the Market Square, where I ordered a bouquet of orange roses to be sent to Barrister S. Maria escorted me to the hotel, we had a little lunch.

"What time do you leave?"

"Probably about nine."

"Will you be in touch?"

"Of course …"

"I hate saying goodbye."

"We won't say goodbye." I said.

"Let's just say, 'Here's looking at you, kid.' *Casablanca*, right?"

I gave her a heartfelt kiss. She walked off at top speed and waved to me from the doorway. Or did I just think she did? I ordered a double whiskey and soon felt like Munch's *Scream*.

⌒   In the afternoon I drifted towards the Limerick again. I was stopped on my way there by a bloodshot man who, temporarily stranded in sobriety, begged two zlotys for some beer. When I gave him five, he said, "Sir, God bless you, you know what a man needs." I thought: this unfortunate carrier of the anguish-and-sorrow virus, he's never seen Marlene Dietrich's legs in *The Blue Angel*, or heard her sing "*Ich bin von Kopf bis Fuß auf Liebe eingestellt*." His Marlene trundled along carrying plastic bags, staggering slightly and mumbling. "In this world," my aunt often pointed out, "injustice wears size XXL."

The man said, "God bless you" again, reached out for the plastic bags from the approaching woman, and ordered her: "Go now, go now."

Karolina's parents were already at the Limerick, with Alexander the artist and several acquaintances and friends.

"Doctor, aren't you sad, leaving us and Kraków?"

"Of course I'm sad, but the fortune teller in the Market Square told me we'll soon see each other again."

"Oh, what a nice fortune teller. Could it be Karolina?"

Alexander gave me one of his prints, a portrait of a woman with her head floating away. His drawings had something of Roland Topor's black humour, which was close to my heart. More and more people joined us, the café filled with dodecaphonic sound, an effect that made me miss the meaning of the words. They faded in the candlelight, stalled mid sentence.

The hubbub triggered off memories of childhood and holidays. Crowds of parents, aunts, relatives, calling out to one another; heavy, lazy suitcases, resistant as recalcitrant dogs. Soulless stations and platforms. The Westbahnhof — my starting point for the Alps — could still remember the deportations to the camps, Maria Callas, the lovers, the young people, and the pensioners.

When I got back to the hotel, the receptionist handed me a buff envelope and said, "A lady left you this."

The padded envelope contained all the old photographs I had looked at with Maria. There was a note: "Please, accept the photos, I'll be happy for you to have them. I've still got the copies. Don't be cross with me. Have a good journey." I phoned Maria.

"Why did you do that? Shouldn't these pictures stay in your granny's restaurant car forever? In Kraków?"

"Let them spend a bit of time in Vienna. One day I'll come for them."

"In that case ... I'll call your bluff."

⌒⌐ Carefully, I took the album out of the envelope. Once again I felt like the author of the *Echoes*: *Thank you for letting me spend a few, inevitable, months in your house. An acquaintance of mine, your friend, had recommended the area. As he always said, it's ideal for lazy mystics. My parched soul wanted to write a book. About love. And tears. "They say, he cried as he kissed her..." I wrote at the rectangular table with the thick linen burgundy tablecloth. If you remember, there was an album on it.*

Photographs guard the past, so I suspect you left it there on purpose.... The first photograph resembled a yellow desert. A woman in a hat. A man in a hat. With a moustache. A little girl with a bow. Caption: "My parents and I, Karlsbad," date illegible. Then more. A slim brunette. Without a hat. Two little girls. Possibly a boy and a girl. Then a woman, but much younger. In a dark dress. Against the background of a funeral parlour. The sign: Norberto de la Riesta. A laughing priest. Sinado Evangelico. Caption: Esmeralda 162. A street. Caption: Rivadavia. A young man is walking north. Light-ing a cigarette, but as if he were hindered by a strong west wind, the pampero. 1928 — a group of young people at a lake, yellowing bulrushes, telegraph poles, with heavy rainclouds in the background. 1928 — the uncertainty of young girls, with the calligraphy of the forest in the background. 1926 — a boat with water still flowing through its wooden veins. 1926 — a young woman, next to her a youth in a sports shirt, airtight space between them. 1927 — the same couple on skis. His arm's around her now. The rusted snow, the corroded caption: "Lvov."

⌒   Text to Doktor. A.: "I've news for you from a reliable source, tomorrow I'm back in Vienna."

He fell upon the town, sudden as sin. He booked into a hotel in St. Mark Street. He registered his name: Jan Sefer. "Must be a Turk or some foreigner, or a mason. Definitely not Polish. A Pole would have a Polish name, wouldn't he? What's he doing in our town, doing nothing? Sometimes he'd pop into the Limerick for a coffee or a glass of green wine. Apparently he ate fog …"

"Can I have the bill, please," I said to the receptionist, who was engrossed in some mathematical thriller.

"Bill or invoice?"

"The bill, I'll pay with a card."

"Will you be leaving us after breakfast?"

"Yes, about nine."

"We hope you enjoyed your stay."

"It was nice, thank you."

He wound a ribbon round his bouquet of phrases. His blazer indicated that he'd lost his appetite and had stopped going to the gym for some time. Irregular blood pressure on top of that, and an accelerated heart rate. A loud group of Italian tourists who'd just arrived must have set off his internal alarm. I could sense the air clotting.

"What else can I do for you?" he asked, handing me my card and receipt.

"That's fine. Have a nice evening," I replied.

He smiled, as my aunt would put it, "without regaining consciousness." Besides, for him the evening was already lost. I had some tea in the restaurant and talked to the waitress for a while.

"My colleague who served you before, he's already left for Ireland," she said.

"We're all of us leaving. And how about you?"

Even though in the stuffy electric light her complexion resembled a bleached cream tablecloth, she blushed. The next moment she was beckoned unceremoniously by a group of cheery men who were apparently enjoying a few days of business-trip freedom, arrogance, and self-assurance. I sensed the acrid odour of sweat and an unpleasant smell of burning. Back in my room I opened my leather Rolls-Royce and started to pack. The table was covered with books, tram tickets, loose change, visiting cards, bills, notes: "Maria," "vocalization," "Handel's epilepsy," "flowers," "Barrister R." The mute TV announced a change in the weather. Streams of rain were flowing on the screen.

꩜   *"Do we ever wonder why the rain falls?" the chemist's daughter asked nobody as she stood in the chemist's shop doorway, watching as streams of hydrogen oxide flowed down the glass. A black Peugeot estate car moved slowly on the muddy road. The headlights penetrated the dark, pushing damp blackness aside. Everybody saw it drive through the town, then turn towards the forest. The chemist's daughter swore there was no one inside.*

꩜   Before I left the room I checked and rechecked the wardrobes and the bathroom. I was careful not to take the toothbrushes, towel slippers, used batteries, ball pens, shoe polish, disposable manicure sets. I put twenty Euros on the table, took a deep breath and, together with my charismatic luggage, made my way to the lift. My dusty Toyota, parked all this time in the small hotel yard, started enthusiastically, relieved we were about to get back on the road. As gleefully as an abandoned dog, it barked its engine into life. Farewell, friends, I said to myself, carefully easing through the tight little streets.

As I approached the A4 motorway, it started to rain. The cloudy sky, not to mention the huge lorries and other speeding monstrosities, filled me with anxiety. Had I left Doktor A. the latest version of my will? I turned on the radio but immediately I crashed into the noisy vexing hubbub of the hit parade. I felt like a lost jockey in a forest of Magritte chessmen. I had to be careful. After all, I was transporting fourteen Kraków days, stored in the memory but still unpacked. I was afraid the events were perishable, that the facts would get lost in transit, that the mind's too fragile. Within a few weeks the colours would fade, the details blur, the voices and the smells disperse. My neurobiologist friends always advised me to use a Dictaphone, keep an audio travel diary. I'd tried many times to confess to my little machine, but with every passing hour I felt resistance growing. The moment the red light — my emblem of readiness and devotion — flashed on, it triggered some unbalanced chemical reactions in my interneuronal connections. A unilateral exchange of opinions? I wasn't too tempted. The mere sight of the Dictaphone made me use primitive sentences, dull language, and it seemed to me I was talking straight into the jaws of a tin wolf that gobbled up the meaning of the words I uttered. I gave it to Susanne in the end, she uses it as an MP3 player.

My thoughts were violently interrupted by the

hooting of a car that was chasing an Opel that was overtaking me. The Opel hooted back and made a gesture, graphically illustrating what he thought about the driver of the Mercedes sitting on his boot. Both cars were smashing the speed limit. In Poland you could easily get rid of all the road signs and white lines, because hardly anyone abided by them. It was the huge trucks and lorries driven by hotheads and daredevils that appalled me most. The hard shoulder was populated by mushroom sellers waving their champignons at us, which — at a hundred and twenty kilometres per hour — could only end in mushroom soup spiced with madness. I also registered a coach parked on the hard shoulder, and a group of urinating citizens turning their backs on the speeding traffic, perfectly at one with the rain and the generally diuretic weather. Perhaps Margot was right and I should have flown?

But in the Czech Republic life went back to normal, and there were even hints of a shy pale blue in the sky. Near Olomouc I stopped at the Zlatá Krupelka Motel and phoned Vlašek.

"*Ahoj, jak se máš?* Where are you?" he yelled cheerfully.

"Drinking coffee at Zlatá Krupelka. I'm not far from Olomouc."

"Spitting distance from me!"

"But I've got to be in Vienna this afternoon. What's the news?"

"We're off to London for a few days. You know us Czechs, everyone from me to Hrabal, we all 'served the King of England.' Where are you coming from?"

"Kraków."

"How did that feel?"

"The only thing missing was a giraffe."

"Interesting. Hadn't they thought of that?"

We arranged for something that's called "next time" and carries the risk of never happening again.

⌒ It was almost 3:00 p.m. when I drove into Vienna. Using a gadget in my car, I listened to the messages on my answerphone. Countless acquaintances, patients, not to mention some friends. Doktor A.: "Is it time to start reheating our meeting?" Susanne: "*Shabriri, Briri, Iri, Ri.*" Maria: "Let me know when you get there. I can't believe we shan't be going into town today together." Some people I met on holiday: "The rain's falling upside down here." And more: "Can Arctic Root ease depression?" A text message: "Got to the Limerick a few minutes after you left. Bad luck? Tomorrow I go to La Gomera for seven days. Uncle Shakespeare says, 'I'm flying to happiness, can't catch me!' Karolina."

⌢⌣   Back in my flat, which Pani Róża had festively prepared, I slept right through the night and far longer than was reasonable. The flat looked like a suit collected from Stross Dry Cleaners' in Hoher Market, still unpacked inside a plastic cloak. My desk was like polished jasper. The windows, left slightly ajar, breathed in the air. I could feel the presence of my beautiful Rafaela leaning across an Italian table, and I even began to suspect Pani Róża hadn't left the house. Was she hiding in the wardrobe? I immediately transferred my suitcase from the hall to the wardrobe, where it stood on guard, protecting my peripatetic imagination. In the kitchen, next to a pile of junk mail, newspapers, and letters neatly arranged on top of each other, I found a note: "I will be out of Vienna for a week, so I have left the other set of keys with Doktor A. I hope you are pleased. See you soon. Róża." I imagined her small town where the air was being grilled and the sweating sun sets in the local pub. Her fiancé, whom she mentioned sometimes, had worked for years on building sites in Germany. They were united by their separation, by their dislike of the countries they illegally worked in, and by national pride blessed by the parish priest. Pani Róża didn't resent spending money on her faith, which needed refurbishment from time to time. Thanks to her, the local church in her little town grew lovelier and lovelier. Her handwriting was neat, but you could see she drew the letters with distrust and disbelief. "See you soon. Róża." I smiled at the short but oh-so-promising sentence.

⌒ "You want to know about Kraków…" Doktor A. and I were sitting in an overflowing café near the Musikverein. Here, 6:00 p.m. mostly attracted concertgoers, lured by the wine or the Satanic espresso. Ladies were still touching up their lips with rosy lipsticks and pearl gloss. After 7:00 p.m., the clientele began to go, leaving in their wake the fragrance of prosperity, harmony, and nutmeg.

"You want to know about Kraków…" I tried to describe the city, its racing pulse and its startling jigsaw architecture. The inscrutable walls, splattered with graffiti, the shoddy jewellery of contemporary junk.

I told him about delicious friends, eccentric encounters, crassness, drunkenness, and shallow dogmatic piety. I told him about the past, it was like mistletoe, a parasite that couldn't detach itself from reality. And about the fact that, just like the mistletoe, the past is medicinal and poisonous too.

"I was living in two different dimensions, and those *Echoes* from Argentina linked them together. Perhaps one day you'll meet Maria, Karolina ..."

"Do they really exist?" A. asked disbelievingly. "Watch out you don't start searching for them, like me with my Argentinean lady — in menus, in towns' names, timetables —"

"Time, you see: nowadays it's an embarrassing secret. Armies of dates either go off to war or retreat. There's no other way."

"Jung, our clinic cat, noticed that ages ago," said Doktor A.

"What do you mean?"

"For some time he's been sleeping exclusively on calendars."

"He'll end up with aggravated date-phobia."

At that point Susanne phoned.

"*Shabriri, Briri, Iri, Ri,*" I heard a joyful voice. "It's great you're back, you've got to meet my Emil."

"Dark hair?"

"Red setter."

"Even better."

"We're beginning to think about the future."

"Dangerous hobby."

"Shut up, cynic."

"Buying a house? Adopting a dog? Off to the Canaries?"

"We're getting married."

"Are you insane? You've still got a few trombone concerts left in you. Listen carefully to *Tannhäuser*, the overture, maybe you'll change your mind. Why the rush?

"Because of love. I want you to be our witness."

"Oh no. Whenever I was a witness, the marriages fell apart. Do you want to take the risk?"

"Did they really?"

"I swear."

"Didn't even *Shabriri* help?"

"It didn't."

I was drawn into her laughter, a sound spraying happiness over fertile Fate.

"I know all about it," said Doktor A. "I've met Emil and I've been to lots of Susanne's concerts. I know nothing about trombones, but it probably reduces our lady colleague's psychophysical stress."

"Really? I trust there's some phonetic-rhythmic therapy too. But does it have to lead to a wedding?"

"Everybody goes fishing at least once a lifetime," Doktor A. summed up.

"Hmm, you reeked of Husserl just now," I said.

"It's not a bad drink."

⌒⌒   In with the mail, a letter from my old friend in Switzerland: "Forgive my cramped style. Most of my astronomically huge correspondence consists of office mail — licences, grants, authors, foundations, stuff like that. Hope your time in Kraków didn't put a strain on your imagination. Maybe you'll write it up? The moving memoirs of a doctor searching for his roots, interviews with yourself, or a sort of fortnight-long autobiography: minipoetical or poetological. When you decide on another insane expedition, warn me. As for me, I've experienced a *lucidum intervallum*: I loaded myself, my depression, Proton the cat, and some real estate into a lorry and went off to Lucerne, a nice and lucid little town. Here my anabiosis begins and ends (from Gk. *anabioun*, to return to life). Cheers." And a short P S.: "I don't know if you know, but B. and I have decided to seal our long-term relationship. With a wedding. B. proposed to me at her friend's funeral, so probably she'll be faithful till the grave."

⌒⌒ "Herr Doktor, could you just pull a few pages out from my memory? I can't shut them up," a nice female patient — I saw her every few months — said to me. She worked for Lufthansa. She always tried to encourage me: "All you need do is book your ticket and check in online." She split up from her husband a few years ago. Her son lived in New York and their contact had shrunk to brief phone conversations. "When I ask him, 'How's life?' he always quotes Milton: 'Better to reign in hell than serve in heaven.' What do you say to that, Herr Doktor?" "He's probably right," I replied. "But he's a waiter, not even the boss of the restaurant." "Now he's a waiter, he'll be the boss later." I tried to cheer her up but to no avail. She brought me tourist leaflets, brochures, catalogues. "Look, this year black's in." I always prescribed fluoxetine, which she regarded as an old friend. She violently rejected all other suggestions with a sudden movement, which invariably pushed my papers off my desk. On the ward, the patients were watching a TV program with a laugh track. Apparently canned laughter was first used in the 1950s in *The Hank McCune Show*, about an incompetent whose attempts to cope with his bad luck landed him in worse trouble. "It's for the less sophisticated," my aunt used to say. "They must be told when to laugh." The forced laughter chased me as I left the hospital, twisting and rolling down the long narrow corridors, infecting the patients with the virus: synthetic joy. Even the evening (it now began in the autumn afternoon) had turned into a joke.

⟳ "I'm dying from curiosity, I'm all ears," said Z. from the Polish bookshop, handing me hot black coffee in a mug.

"I ought to start with the weather. Well, the weather was well-meaning. If it rained, it was through absent-mindedness. The temperature was roughly…raspberry sorbet."

"Raspberry? You're sure?"

"Absolutely."

"Quite a tasty temperature for the time of year."

"I agree. Now I should move on to: travel. Driving a car through Poland requires a lot of courage."

"I always believed in you!"

"I wasn't disappointed by the Park Hotel. Tactful breakfasts, soft-boiled eggs, my favourite, rye bread, white cheese. An intriguing trio of waiters. Like storks flying away for the winter."

"Pure poetry already, Herr Doktor."

"They coped bravely with the sleepless dawn. They always served the words on the right, with a white serviette.... End of poem."

"Fantastic."

"And what's next? Do you want to know what's next?"

"I'd rather know what came before."

"Before? Black holes. Narrow uneven pavements receding underfoot. You have to master a new walking technique. Beyond that, lots of fans of vodka and expressive language — but I shan't quote."

"Lucky me."

"It's strange, you know: there's religion hanging from almost every washing line, but there's not much faith."

"I think you exaggerate, Herr Doktor."

"Of course I exaggerate. Poland's suspicious, distrustful, explosive. Hardly anyone will say hello to you, in the lift, on the stairs.... Why are you smiling?"

"Because the dessert's coming next, I bet."

"Exactly. Now I'll tell you about a wonderful city and my mesmeric meetings."

"Fantastic."

"I'm not going to tell you about the past, because you know all that already. But at least I've left the cemetery door ajar. My father's pleased, I think.... Oh, my aunt materialized as usual, like a peace envoy for the EU."

The story of my journey took almost two hours. I lost myself in digressions, complex plots, minor episodes. I kept recalling insignificant details: a brass doorknob intruding into a hotel room, a persistent stain on a restaurant tablecloth, crags of clouds, the posters at the Limerick.

"Fantastic." Z. summed it up. "I'm proud of you."

"I brought you a present. An angel thermometer in traditional Krakovian dress."

"Amazing! I'm so proud of you."

After I left the bookshop, I got a text from Karolina: "Greetings from the isle of La Gomera. Christopher Columbus sends love too."

A telephone call from Maria. It made me realize that my visit to Kraków had shattered her peace of mind. Mira's death was dying in her again. My aunt, brutally: "Somebody's always dying for someone."

"I can't come home from your trip," Maria said, "I miss you."

"The brighter side of our dark side," I said weakly, "is that what's done's done."

"Are you sure? What's done? We only exchanged a few words, and we went to a graveyard. Memory's last stop," she added darkly. "Or is it like a tram loop?"

"Things like this get rusted over the phone. Come here."

"I'm going to some friends next week. In Arizona. They work at an observatory near Tucson."

"Be careful. That's where the meteors crash."

"Listen to me: her life was extinguished like a meteor.... That sounds quite good, doesn't it?"

"How long will you go for?"

"I should tell you, 'My whole lifetime,' but that means a month."

"What should I wish you?"

"A good trip."

"So I wish you a good trip. But you know, don't you, that I'm wishing you —"

"Stop, Herr Doktor. I've got to tell you about these Clarks shoes. They're wonderfully comfortable, never leave my feet. Good night, take care."

"You too.... We'll talk about Vienna another time."

I heard the faint click of the phone being put down. I poured myself a small whiskey and started feeling guilty about the flood in India, Hurricane Ike off the Texas coast, and the collapse of the world stock market.

There was something I had overlooked in this case. I'd checked out of Maria too quickly, I'd handled her like an object in Kraków's collection of precious china. Had she fallen in love with me? Had I brushed the lock from her forehead in an ambiguous way? Was I too lyrical when I fastened the buttons on her coat? My aunt: "And can dust return to life?"

◯ "*Shabriri, Briri, Iri, Ri.*" A meeting with Susanne and her friend F., who worked for Austrian Airlines and whom I'd not seen for a while. I thought she'd grown a few centimetres.

"Well, I'm two millimetres taller every flight."

F. came from Poland, Kraków in fact, and she ate up my stories. She was the spitting image of Jeanne Samary, the flame-red French actress Renoir so often painted. F. dressed in elegant browns adorned with jewellery in the very best of taste. A warm, sunny autumn walked in with her. I used to visit her family in Grinzing many years ago. We swapped books. I remember the bookshelf. Sholem Asch's *A String of*

Pearls. Michael Walzer's *On Toleration.* Gombrowicz's *Cosmos.* And *The Mushroom Atlas* with a red toadstool on the front. The girls were in great spirits.

I asked, "Your next flight's to — ?"

"The hairdresser's."

"Scheduled?"

"Maybe you don't know," Susanne intercepted. "F.'s just got married. To an Indian diplomat."

"Congratulations. I've always said the world began with a mixed marriage."

As I watched, they blended into one harmonious whole with a tapestry of burgundy leaves that was climbing a wooden fence.

∽ Doktor A. on the phone: "Will you drop by for some Spirit of Lourdes? A patient gave me a bottle. Seems it's 40 percent revelation."

∽ I returned to the Kraków theme during a supper with the Beneks. And at my father's grave. I spoke to Father in an undertone, so as not to scare off the leaves surfing on granite slabs. "I had a glimpse

of a very good dream. Now the dream belongs to you."
"Amen," my aunt added. "Drink an even number of
glassfulls, then you'll sleep well."

A slim brunette caught my eye, wearing an allusion
to a skirt, so short it was almost absent. She stood by
the next grave. She smiled at the black granite. On it
lay a bunch of irises tied with a man's yellow tie. Geo-
metrically patterned black stockings climbed up her
legs, which were extended by high heels that, lacking
a lifeboat, were slowly sinking into the clay. She turned
her head slightly leftwards and I noticed the bright
red, greasy gloss of her lips. She looked the picture
of infidelity. She adjusted the yellow tie and, leaning
over the irises, murmured to herself and burst out
laughing. She sank deeper and deeper into the dank
soil, she seemed a torpedoed ship bound inevitably for
the bottom. Somehow we left the cemetery at the same
moment and got into our cars, I into my Toyota, she
into a silver Lexus. Our doors uttered a similar muffled
sound. Our engines started in unison like a church
choir. She drove ahead of me, occasionally braking.
Red lights, red lips. "Was she cheating on him?" Un-
consciously I was trailing the Lexus, the accidental
witness of my undefined imaginings. Back in the centre,
near the Opera, she drove into the underground car

park while I, after stopping briefly at the Sacher Hotel, went to my clinic. "Was she cheating on him?" I asked Doktor A. "Did Nobel," he quipped, "invent dynamite?"

⌒ December descended on my sullen car park. The Christmas factory geared up. Our concierge parked a few deranged Santas, who waved at us every time the entrance gate opened. Amidst the concrete and the tires dangling over the cars, there were coloured fairy lights now. In harmony with the festive season, sensors and photo cells flashed. The New Year loomed again, the cogs of January were about to grind. My mail box was ravenous for fresh bills, cheques, bank statements. And it was around that time that I was phoned more often than usual by Ida, my ex-wife.

"How are you?"

"Like a Rosenthal dinner service dumped at the pawn-broker's."

"Has something happened?"

"Haven't you heard? World War III."

"You never change," Ida said, resigned. "Evidently you went to Kraków."

"I've finally taken the prescription."

"And how was it?"

"No great side effects. But I'll tell you everything."

"I hope."

"And you?"

"Oh, just life.... I get low sometimes. I mean, everything's fine, possibly even better than fine."

∽ My aunt: "Follow your wife's advice. Fall into Gehenna."

∽ With the Beneks: at the legendary Marchfelderhof, the Viennese Palace of Food. The culinary extravaganza. The astonishing interiors, the baroque excess, everything covered with weapons, medals, photographs, musical instruments, porcelain figurines, bombast. Operatic toilets and melodramatic food. Kitsch, yes, but top-notch. It's a joke at mankind's expense. Cockades, vintage tulle, all the pageantry of our trite nostalgia. Roast venison in chestnut sauce, crayfish-tail cocktails, and ribs that taste of the Brandenburg Concerto at the table where Karajan, Empress

Sissi, and Yehudi Menuhin used to sit. The place's motto: "Each guest is our king, our emperor." We were at the Volksoper Ballet table, with Teresa sitting in for the ballerina Maya Plisetskaya. It smelled of Degas paintings, pork and beef. There was Margot with her aesthetic jewellery. Benek the director-choreographer. Teresa and I grappling with the greasy libretto, making shy attempts to sing. We managed, even though vocalizing's not my forte. We talked about Poland, about its dichotomies, about mutual friends. Kraków was receding from me, escaping into the icy landscapes of Hendrick Avercamp (1585–1634). "When I look at his paintings, I skid," Doktor A. told me at an Amsterdam exhibition.

"What's new in the Kraków chicken-coop?" Margot asked.

"They're clucking about the Crisis, about Worldly Vanity, and they dream of living forever."

"They've got the chance now!" Benek tossed in some news, "We've discovered the longevity gene!"

"It's most probably located," I muttered, "inside these ribs."

"Have you seen the Van Gogh show yet?" Margot asked.

"Yes, and in funny circumstances. Doktor A. and I were invited to the relaunch of one of the Vienna banks.

It was in the Albertina Museum and they combined it with a private viewing of the Van Gogh. They treated us to upbeat speeches insisting that the bank's alive and kicking and awaiting new customers. Considering the Crisis, we felt we were on the Titanic with our life jackets back in the car. But we still managed to see the exhibition and fit in several glasses of rather good wine. As for Van Gogh, I do appreciate him but don't really like him. Which is better, the pork?"

"The beef's quite good too," Benek said.

"Sticking an exhibition in front of people like that!" Margot commented.

Waiters, ambassadors of the empire of consumption, kept proposing a cornucopia of culinary treats. They teased our taste buds, coaxed us into trying a smidgeon of spicy shrimp cream sauce or else some sweet perversion. They were in a trance. Tempting, cajoling, urging, passion sparkling in their eyes, they catalogued their opulent puddings and the vivid drinks. Their sweating faces and shaking hands said, "You've got to partake in the civilization show with bulimic enthusiasm!"

"Thank you, not just now," Benek disciplined the servile troops.

"After this meal," I said, "we're all headed for extinction."

"Even without the meal," Margot added.

"And this is the way the world ends, not with a bang, but a binge."

I liked the Beneks, I adored Margot. In their presence, time slowed. We sipped the fragility of life, we nibbled utopia.

⌒⌒ The world financial crisis did not spare Pani Róża. I noticed her falling into economic melancholia.

"I shouldn't have changed my Euros into zlotys," she said sadly, tossing back the hair from her eyes. "What's it come to? My fiancé says someone's making money from it."

"Some fiend. But I'm sure there's a financial guardian angel looking after you, Róża. Me, I've lost my suitcase key. Now it's locked for centuries."

"Honestly?" Pani Róża was horrified.

"I'm not joking. I'll have to call Louis Vuitton in Paris, but I'm afraid they'll fob me off with a bottle of cognac instead of the key."

"Then hadn't we better look for it?"

"I already have, lots of times."

"Then we've got to turn to St. Anthony."

"He's your friend, maybe you should try."

"How much can we give him?"

"The whole Federal Reserve Bank. The one that's added so much to your misery."

Pani Róża wasn't convinced I'd given her the right answers, and I went out, leaving her wondering.

⌢⌢   On the way I got a text from Karolina: "You've forgotten me, Mister." I wrote back: "Not at all, I've just been busy sex-changing and, as your uncle would say, the rest is silence." Karolina, that evening: "So are you my girlfriend now?" My reply: "Just the opposite, I'm twice as much a man." Karolina, moments later: "Here in Poland ambiguity's risky." Doktor A.: "You cannot go on seducing juveniles." Aunt: "Remember, ten cubits of speech were sent unto the world; women took nine of them, and they left the men one."

⌢⌢   News reached me at the hospital that my Swiss friend was dead. "He died the way he was born," his wife said emotionally, "with a cry. Suddenly there was

a pain in his heart....Will you come to Zurich?" "I will."
A. said to me: "Knowing him, he meant it as a joke but it
went wrong."

"Something's wrong if it's dawn at sunset."

⌒ I took a morning flight to Zurich. They had
scheduled the funeral for 1:00 p.m. "Philosophy doesn't
look its best in the sun," my Swiss friend used to say.
At a time like this, it's better cloaked in darkness. I used
to come to this city a lot; a close friend (female) ran an
art gallery in its very heart, near Bahnhofstrasse. I liked
to have my morning coffee while I leafed through the
Neue Zürcher Zeitung. I used to listen out for the city's
High Alemannic dialect; it was slowly disappearing,
sucked into the multilingual abyss. Raucous fast foods,
McDonald's and kebabs were driving out the elegance
of past times that had been tailored to fit Thomas Mann
and Max Frisch. Maybe in the Canton of Grisons, up
in the forests of the Alps, you can still meet Friedrich
Nietzsche's headache out on a hike, but I was being
sucked back into the city again. The Indian taxi driver
took me from the airport to the Uetliberg cemetery
with its beautiful panorama of Lake Zurich and the

encircling hills. There was already a little crowd there: a slab of black, a monolith of whispers and conversations and even laughter. Refreshed and straight from the beauty parlour, the widow welcomed the guests. She offered her hand or, as in my case, her cheek to kiss.

"I'm so glad you've come, he needs you."

Suddenly some motorbikes roared past. It was a trick of my friend's ghost, as if he were saying: "Will you look at yourselves? You're all making eyes at my silly wife. She'd be happier watching the new Woody Allen. You're all looking forward to a cardboard lunch with her — 'We cater for your individual needs: banquets, picnics, funerals' — and me, I'm just lucky I'm dead. As a heap of ashes I don't have to join in your indigestible fun. Remembering the past's a waste of time, my friend. Quick as you can, run!" A small urn was talking to me. I gaped disbelievingly at it. "In circumstances like these, Herr Doktor, how'm I supposed to hang on to my wits?"

"Won't you stay?"

"I'm sorry, I've got to be in Vienna today."

Graveyard whispers stuck to my shoes, disguised as rotting leaves and clods of clay.

At Zurich Airport a charter flight to the Canaries

was checking in. The holiday mood in the queue. Bold hats made of see-through fabrics, from corduroy, cotton, and linen; straw hats tied round with rainbow ribbons. A makeover for a cold December. I was deadly tired. A stewardess, smiling at me: "Have a nice flight." On board: "Good evening, this is your Austrian Airlines captain speaking … We shall be flying at the height of … The flying time to Vienna will be one hour and … The temperature in Vienna is …" In the plane's roaring toilet I couldn't recognize my face. I asked the stewardess for a shot of vodka and watched as the lights of Vienna-Schwechat Airport blossomed.

"What can you do with death, so that it dies quicker?"

I scoured the airport car parks for my car. It was cold, damp, and smelled of mould. I switched on the engine and slowly moved towards the city.

⌒⊃ My aunt: "If the house collapses, pity the windows."

⌒⊃ In the memory of a young student I discover several pieces of relevant data. The dominant father;

repressed emotions, punishments, and demands; the absent mother. The longing for a lover-mother.

"Can you help me, Herr Doktor?"

He was fragile as glass, like cracking ice.

"Yes, I can…"

A postcard from Maria: "Hello from the Grand Canyon. The Lord had a good day when he created this bit of the Earth. Hope you're well? Me too. Rilke was right: we're a fragment of Nothing."

∽ My loss-making laziness gene made me put off some things till tomorrow. Our stuffy little room was like an oven. But Susanne looked refreshed. She explained to me that Saint Géran, the French spring water, contains zero bacteria.

"Happiness," I said, "has taken your brains away. And besides, I love bacteria."

"Music-loving bacteria," I added after a while.

Susanne continued to smile at me, with those braces on her teeth, and rescheduled my appointments. The lady from Lufthansa, whose appointment I couldn't change, entertained me with a quote from Oscar Wilde, or was it Karl Kraus: "One of the most common of all diseases is diagnosis." I suspected that apart from the medication I prescribed for her, she also swallowed several aphorisms and quotations daily, to surprise me with. The overheated radiators made her cheeks flush, double strength.

And finally that afternoon, a beer with Doktor A.

"Don't ask me about anything today," I said.

"I wasn't going to. But I have to tell you, Benek couldn't get through to you, they've gone to Venice."

"It's a corpse of a city."

"Profitable corpse, though. Pani Róża told me your suitcase story."

"If she's got time to talk about my suitcase, it's a sign the Polish zloty's gone up."

"Exactly the opposite, it's down."

It was getting darker, the streetlamps came on. Light poured out from billboards, fluorescent adverts, shop windows, headlights — it ranged from gentle, dim, and atmospheric up to blindingly sharp. The wind announced rain.

I asked Doktor A.: "Is it time for a flu jab?"

He replied: "I see your neuronal activity's back to normal."

Back in my flat, I tidied up the books and finally found my aunt's favourite, *The Cultural History of*

Operetta, by Bernard Grun. I'd been looking for it for an age. My aunt, satirical-critical operetta personified, could always listen for hours to the frivolous melodies that my father despised. Carrying on cleaning, I packed all the old newspapers into a cardboard box and went to the trash area, where I bumped into my obsessional neighbour. She used every such opportunity to warn me against strokes, diseases, floods, and bankruptcy.

"I can't sleep. I'm scared I'll die in my sleep."

"And?"

"And what? Isn't that bad enough, Herr Doktor?"

"It could be worse."

I helped her put her stuff into the correct containers, accompanied by the clinking of bottles, the rustling of paper, and then the slam of the door. We wished each other goodnight and as she got in the lift, I said:

"Don't worry. Go to sleep, you won't die tonight."

My newly tidied bookshelf made me think of Stanislaw Lem. If you replaced the book in his anecdote with a man, then each new man would push another man into a giant bin. You could only console yourself with the fact that Homer was there already, lying in that bin.

I poured myself a glass of red wine and reached for the Inevitable, i.e., my desk diary. I wrote in the new appointments, answered some unimportant phone calls, looked through the post.

From faraway Australia, an ex-patient had written to me: "Truth doesn't answer many questions. Besides, it's always got an alibi." I looked into the dark window. *"There was a toucan sitting on the window sill."* If I were to write a novel, that might be the last sentence ...

AFTERWORD

Ewa Lipska was born in 1945 in Kraków, Poland. She was a leading member of the generation of oppositional East European poets in the late 1960s and 1970s. Much of her work was published clandestinely by the underground press. In her poetry, language was put under the microscope, analyzed, and stripped of pretence: she exposed the underlying anxieties of institutions and individuals alike. Following the fall of Communism, she became Poland's cultural representative in Vienna, and she now lives both in Vienna and Kraków. Her first novel, *Sefer*, was published in Poland in 2009.

While she was with the Polish embassy in Austria, Ewa Lipska was assigned to work with the Simon Wiesenthal Dokumentationszentrum. The centre's massive archive collection — which Wiesenthal had assembled over half a century through his own researches and via correspondence from witnesses and victims around the world — was about to be digitized. It included letters, manuscripts, a library, over 8,000 files on Holocaust perpetrators, and some 35,000 photographic images. "That's where I encountered the 'reality' of the past," Ewa Lipska recalls. "My conversations with S.W. about politics, about the pattern of history — they were a fountain of knowledge for me." This collaboration became a friendship that lasted until Wiesenthal's death in 2005. He helped to inspire the character of Jan Sefer's deceased father, who provides the novel with its plot motor. When we talked to her while working on the translation, Ewa said, "All of us, regardless of our historical situations, are hunting for our past.... We'll always be talking it through with our psychotherapists, with historians — today's detectives."

On one level, then, *Sefer* begins like a thriller, with a son entrusted with a mission to investigate the past. This will involve a journey away from apparent security, and in fact this is a novel in which the hunter slowly senses that he may be pursuing himself. Dr. Sefer's thoughts and experiences begin to shadow, even merge with, those of both the mysterious author of the *Echoes* and his own father. A "pretty good love affair" (or was it a "pretty great" one?) that happened seventy years before happens again (or does it, quite?). "It's only memories that help my protagonists to meet," Lipska stresses. "The past gives them a kick, it acts as an aphrodisiac, connects them." This is not a novel "haunted" by the past: "The past is crucial if we're to understand the Now." Some of the photographs described in *Sefer* are of Ewa Lipska's own family. But not all. "Different times overlap," she says. "I'm always amazed by the similarity of people's fates.... There's a sepia mist that binds our memory together.... We long for something else, for a time that doesn't exist, but perhaps did once." In *Sefer*, memories fade, memories change and intermingle, and memories can be retouched like photographs so that "we become more beautiful, more distinct, almost flawless — but not true anymore." The past is elliptical, enigmatic, and intangible, and yet for Lipska this is simply a fact of life: "What is tragic to me is the fact that humanity doesn't draw conclusions from history."

Sefer is also a travelogue, a tale of two cities. "Kraków and Vienna were both woven into the Austro-Hungarian empire," Lipska points out, but the history of the Polish city — not least the fate of its Jewish population — has created a very different shape and texture. We travel with Sefer from the concert halls, plush cafés, and comfortable clinics of Vienna, along the battered roads of what used to be Communist Czechoslovakia and Poland, into Kraków — a space of scruffy intimacy, where hotel staff tell you their dreams. Deftly, Lipska evokes Kraków's rich yet traumatic Christian-Jewish heritage, but she also introduces a teeming, vivid community with a voracious hunger for the future. In Kraków's narrow streets — in images as fragmented as in a broken mirror and via snatches of dialogue half-heard in the hubbub — Sefer meets a crowd of intriguing personalities who stimulate and somehow reflect aspects of himself. Ewa Lipska leaves open the question: how therapeutic is this journey?

In Sefer's cultured circle, wit holds emotion at bay and identity is elusive. Sefer's father avoids discussing his past. Present-day romances are to be talked about rather than lived. Though many of Sefer's friends in Vienna and elsewhere are Polish or have Polish links, they regard the country with nervous irony, from a distance. But of course Dr. Sefer is a psychoanalyst; the surface of his world of almost non-stop banter is repeatedly disrupted by the startling comments of his patients — as paradoxical and confronting as the surreal vision of the *Echoes* and the Talmudic inter-ruptions of his aunt: they propel him on his journey.

Sefer is a quest without closure, a love story that never approaches consummation or commitment, and a novel whose focus shifts alongside Jan Sefer's own shifts in focus and concentration. Its form suggests levels of consciousness, the acknowledged and the suppressed, and it registers, too, the amorphous com-plexity of our own contemporary experience: how are questions of personal identity affected by events beyond our control? While Sefer journeys into the past and the Poles imagine their futures in and beyond the New Europe, the massive financial crisis from which we still have not recovered is happening, as it were, just off camera.

The novel is cinematic, offering us fleeting images of broken cobbles, an arcane number on the front of a tram, an exotic street name in a photograph, a Van Gogh painting surrounded by bankers. This is the cinema of memory, though, where the documentary and the dream, like the living and the dead, are equally substantial, and at any moment new streets, new photographs, and other people's stories may beckon us into them. And *Sefer* is richly scored: "I suspect that perhaps music's important for Dr. Sefer because he's my alter ego," Lipska explains. "Music's very important for me. It protects me from crashing into the world. That's why I often visited the Musikverein in Vienna, the Konzerthaus, and everywhere else where there were concerts and music events. Whenever I can, wherever I am, I escape into concert halls. When the words aren't enough, it's worthwhile reaching for the music."

Sefer is the author's alter ego, too, in that this is a novel perhaps only a poet could write, but a poet who distrusts rhetoric, who knows that language both constructs and fails us. *Sefer* demonstrates language's artifice, its gift for evasion, but also celebrates its precision. Its poetry is encased and grounded in the sensuous descriptions of food, drink, architecture, scents, sounds and tactility. But — as we have found as translators, working on Ewa Lipska's poetry since the late 1980s — at any moment her language will burst all certainties apart. In the dreamlike text the *Echoes*, apparently written in Poland but posted from a magic-realist dimension called "Argentina" ("If you haven't been to the end of the world, you know nothing"), the repressed returns and falls upon a little town "like sin," shattering logic with each sentence and opening the unconscious.

We hear of a camp survivor, a patient at the clinic, who tells his doctor all his experiences and then announces: "You're cured. I can do no more." Ewa Lipska doesn't confirm the healing powers of memories or texts or of the talking cure, but *Sefer* repeatedly stresses that the listener is as important as the speaker, the reader as the writer.

Sefer watches young people, "still free from the torment of ambiguity and uncertainty"; Karolina tells him, "Ambiguity's risky." But in *Sefer* all stories feed uncertainty, and must. Sefer is on a journey. And Sefer, like *Sefer*, is unfinished.

BB & TH

RECYCLED
Paper made from
recycled material
FSC® C103567

Marquis Book Printing Inc.

Québec, Canada

2012

Printed on Silva Enviro 100% post-consumer EcoLogo certified paper,
processed chlorine free and manufactured using biogas energy.